The Talbott Agreement was a deadly new twist to the world balance of power—a plan so fantastic that even the President of the U.S. found it hard to believe . . .

But the Red Chinese believed it. And to counteract the effects of the Talbott Agreement, they unveiled a secret thought control weapon that threatened the destruction of mankind.

There was only one way to stop the deadly onslaught of terror—repudiate the Agreement and capture the scientist who masterminded the powerful Chinese weapon.

There was only one man for the job—secret agent and China specialist Jim Moser, who had to work on both sides of the Bamboo Curtain to prevent a world-wide nuclear holocaust.

THE TALBOTT
AGREEMENT

Richard M. Garvin

and

Edmond G. Addeo

AWARD BOOKS
NEW YORK

TANDEM BOOKS
LONDON

FIRST AWARD PRINTING 1969

To Fred Kerner

On this mountain there are no trees
In this river no water flows
In this place the people cannot weep
AI CH'ING

Copyright © 1968 by Richard M. Garvin and Edmond G. Addeo
Published by arrangement with Sherbourne Press, Inc.

Library of Congress Catalog Number 68-55591

AWARD BOOKS are published by
Universal Publishing and Distributing Corporation
235 East Forty-fifth Street, New York, N. Y. 10017

TANDEM BOOKS are published by
Universal-Tandem Publishing Company Limited
14 Gloucester Road, London SW7, England

Manufactured in the United States of America

CHAPTER ONE

DATE: August 4, 1969
TIME: 12:00 noon
PLACE: The Taklamakan Desert in the Tarim Basin, northwest China

*　　*　　*

Chang Kwok-wah closed his eyes for a moment and pressed two fingers of each hand against the burning lids. Then he focused again on the shimmering horizon, searching through the refracting waves that rose from the barren grey sand.

It was a perfect place for the test, a perfect day. But the ninety degree heat surged through Chang's blue linen *Jem-ming,* prickled his skin with heat rash, made him twist and turn uncomfortably as he searched for a tiny speck in the hot, greenish sky.

Chang sat on a crowded grandstand hastily constructed of birchwood. Nearby was a new and polished Soviet-built bus, its radiator still hissing as wisps of steam curled from beneath the hood. But that was all. Beyond the island of linen-clad notables on the rickety bleachers nothing lived, nothing moved.

Beside Chang Kwok-wah sat Dr. Tsien Hsue-shen, the quietly spectacular nuclear scientist—now turned psychologist—who had repatriated from the United States of America fifteen years before. Next to Tsien sat K'ang Sheng, the aging, willowy director of the ruthless Social Affairs Department, the Party's euphemistically titled security intelligence network. Two rows above them were Lin Piao, the government's defense minister, China's premier Chou En-lai, and between them, frowning sullenly as he wiped away the droplets of oily sweat with the

5

sleeve of his undecorated *Jem-ming,* Chairman Mao Tse-tung, a paper fan waving listlessly in his chubby hand.

They and the cluster of top officials around them had all been baked and jostled during the last sixty-five miles from Lop Nor, crammed in the unmarked red-and-white-trimmed bus. And now, eighteen hundred miles from Peking, their discomfort was hardly eased by the thin canvas canopy that deflected the scalding sun, and the hot air bristled with a belligerence, with an unspoken challenge that said "Show us."

Chairman Mao had insisted that all the highest political and military figures join him in witnessing the curious demonstration about to take place, despite his own measure of incredulity. It was a convincing indication of its importance and a singular honor for Chang and Dr. Tsien. And yet, to Chang, it seemed as if the assembled dignitaries were watching him instead of the burning sky; that he was the object of skepticism from what was perhaps the most concentrated collection of ruthless power ever gathered on earth.

But that, after all, was only natural. For it had been Chang and the uncompromising Dr. Tsien, almost alone, who had brought five years of research to this auspicious climax. They were the prime creators of a new architecture for creative defense that transcended science. They were not only the inventors of an awesome weapon; they were actually a part of the weapon itself.

There were very few others who knew. Aside from a handful of particularly adept students at the University of Peking and a handful of K'ang Sheng's personal henchmen, only the assembled officials here in the desert had access to their tightly wound wheel of secrecy. True, there had been the technicians who had helped to design and assemble the simple black cabinet that sat in front of the grandstand. But they knew nothing of its purpose or its operation, knew only that it was a kind of amplifier—but one capable of amplifying nothing that they could know or understand.

Of all of Red China's clandestine projects, this one was perfect in its impenetrable security. The key to the mystery was one that required no elaborate factories for its production, no neon-lighted laboratories cluttered with scientists, no endless discussions or blackboard computations, no notes, no memos, no formulae—nothing that might fall into the wrong hands. And about this, at least, Chairman Mao was greatly pleased.

Chang glanced back at Mao from time to time, watched him as he sipped on the endless supply of black-market Coca-Cola his aides provided, speaking occasionally to Chou, who would answer through a haze of yellow cigarette smoke, or to Lin Piao, who would always nod in automatic agreement.

Then Chang peered again at the sky and gently nudged Dr. Tsien. He pointed toward the horizon, indicating a tiny pinprick that danced through the heat-fragmented sky. Tsien nodded and called out to the group in rapid *Kuo-yu,* his native Mandarin dialect.

"If the esteemed comrades will now put on their protective helmets and goggles, please, the demonstration will commence." Then Chang joined him as he moved to the two low stools placed directly in front of the black cabinet. They simultaneously reached for a pair of plastic helmets that hung on the cabinet. They were the shape and size of laboratory bell jars, silvered on the inside, and connected to the cabinet by single, thick cables. And as they exchanged the helmets for their olive-drab caps, they suddenly became two headless robots, plugged into an ominous black machine.

Chang began to control his breathing as he strained to look out through the silvered surface of the helmet. He tensed as the crowd grew quiet and the black pinprick grew into a silver needle that pierced higher into the sky. In seconds the fighter drone would come screaming overhead, skimming low across the scorched sand at 450 miles an hour. And his quiet confidence almost wavered as he saw it begin to take form—a powerful and invincible machine, daring and challenging, the product of five years of constant labor.

He knew the plane intimately, of course. He had been present when it was carefully tested and inspected before many of the officials present. It was a standard aircraft, tested in battle against all the bullets and missiles China's enemies could assemble. It was thoroughly armored, but empty of any weapons or explosive materials. Even its supply of kerosene fuel was carefully metered to be at a low point as it streaked over the grandstand on its programmed course. It was now merely a projectile, streaking toward a target in the desert a few miles beyond them.

Tsien made a small adjustment of the single control knob on the cabinet, deftly bringing the needle on the large dial to ten. The Chinese characters on the dial read: *mao—pao—li—lian,* which translated roughly to "brainwave strength units." Then Chang heard his voice whisper tensely through the miniaturized intercom in the helmet. "Ready. Now!"

Chang's body suddenly tensed; his eyes strained toward a slice of empty sky a few hundred yards ahead of them until the ringing in his own ears matched the scream of the onrushing jet.

And then it was upon them. One moment a screaming silver bird and then, perhaps a picosecond later, a ball of orange fire that paled the sun, that swelled and contracted as it passed overhead, then darkened and dispersed in a cloud of micron-sized dust particles, harmlessly, formlessly drifting to the desert sands beyond.

Chang felt himself trembling as he watched the settling black dust. Now that it was over, now that they had proved in practice what had only been tested before on tiny models, he could enjoy the luxury of the pride his doubts and fears had concealed. He forgot the searing heat and his almost continuous fatigue, and smiled openly as he heard the group around him break into exclamations of amazement and admiration and finally a round of soft applause.

Then he wiped the sweat from his forehead as he felt the strong hand of Dr. Tsien pat him warmly on the back, turned to exchange mutual congratulations and watch as Chairman Mao beamed down at them, offering a pleased salute with his Coca-Cola. Premier Chou raised his hand in approval and, though his face remained fixed and expressionless, Lin Piao nodded twice.

Several minutes later another dot unfolded on the horizon. This time it loomed up high and noiseless in the western sky—a huge delta-winged bomber of the type being developed for long-range nuclear capability. It, too, was a computer-controlled drone. It, too, was stripped of ammunition and excess fuel. And it was miles instead of feet above them.

Chang and Dr. Tsien repeated their performance in front of the black cabinet. Under the silver helmets, their smiles dissolved into intense concentration and finally into taut, frightening grimaces as the aircraft passed under the sun. Then, almost directly overhead, there was no longer an aircraft, but the same fireball and a puff of dust. No explosion. Not even an audible sound, but merely a feeling of pressure that seemed to press the rickety grandstand closer to the desert sand.

And there, in the blistering heat, Chang Kwok-wah felt his initial relief and pleasure turn to dread, felt the prickly heat turn to tingles of ice that danced unseen beneath his blue *Jem-ming.*

* * *

DOSSIER: TSIEN HSUE-SHEN
  DATE OF BIRTH: 13 Oct 09   HEIGHT: 5 ft. 2 in.
  PLACE OF BIRTH: Shanghai, China WEIGHT: 142 lbs.
  MARITAL STATUS: Married   HAIR: Black
  NATIONALITY: Chinese National EYES: Brown
  (see below)
  Education: Nanyang Primary School; Nanyang Middle School; University of Communications (Chao-tung tai shui); Engineering degree; MS Aeronautical Engineering; PhD, Aeronautical Engineering, Massachusetts Institute of Technology; M.S. Psychology, Boston University
  PARENTAL BACKGROUND: Father: Tsien Yit-tung, occupation unknown; deceased. Mother: Wei Lee-su, occupation unknown; deceased.
  PHYSICAL CHARACTERISTICS: Receding hairline; round face with pockmarks on cheeks; eyes set close together;

wears glasses. No known scars or birthmarks. No physical examination on record.

BACKGROUND COMMENTARY: Had a middle-class upbringing in Shanghai; was a brilliant student through primary and middle schools in Shanghai, receiving an Engineering degree at the University of Communications in Shanghai. Entered the United States at age 25, 7 June 34, and immediately matriculated Massachusetts Institute of Technology, Cambridge, Mass. Earned Master's degree in 1935, doctorate in Aeronautical Engineering in 1937. Summer schools throughout this tenure, earning Master's in Psychology at Boston University. This subject remained his avocation throughout U.S. residence.

Accepted teaching position on the faculty of California Institute of Technology, Pasadena, Calif., 8 Apr 38. In 1941 his movements restricted because of war effort and his classified projects in aeronautical development at the University. Restrictions lifted, 1943, when government enlisted his aid on nuclear projects, viz., Manhattan. This completed, he was shifted to early rocket research at Cal Tech, and worked briefly with Heinrich von Reichling, Werner Studt, R. Klaus Krupp and other postwar repatriates from Peenemunde rocket site.

Tsien became consultant in 1947 to defense contractors North American Aviation, Inc., Lockheed Aircraft, and Antares Electronics. During this time, Tsien was awarded many commendations and government citations for his vital work in rocket development.

Was offered directorship of newly formed Guggenheim Foundation's jet propulsion research centers in 1949 and accepted such post at California Institute of Technology. Prior to this acceptance, Tsien requested and was granted permission to visit relatives on the Communist-held Chinese mainland. He returned with a wife, Yen-ching.

Tsien became target for Communist-oriented investigation committees in Washington, D.C. and was arrested 6 Mar 51 on conspiracy charges. He was subsequently cleared. However, grew restless in his work and bitterness was noted by government agents at Cal Tech. Federal Bureau of Investigation agents withheld clearances for classified projects.

Newly-formed Aerojet-General Corp. (operating under renowned rocket research scientist von Kármán, near Sacramento, Calif.) accepted Tsien as consultant on privately developed rocket engine techniques in 1952. Immigration authorities seized Tsien's personal notes, diagrams, sketches, and manuscripts upon his attempt to ship them to Aerojet. Deportation papers were prepared and his belongings held, pending further Communist affiliation investigations. Restrictions again lifted in 1953, but Immigration Dept. claimed no knowledge of whereabouts of his technical papers. FBI arrangement in this incident and location of aforementioned papers are still under UMBRELLA.

Subject at this time made no secret of intention to return to China, and government's treatment of him in the United States caused his resignation from all duties. Immediately upon final lifting of travel restrictions from Immigration Dept., Tsien and wife sailed for the Red Chinese mainland 3 Feb 54.   END

—Compiler: Col. Jesse Levarsky
USAF: AO 43348594
22 May 60

DOSSIER ADDENDUM

Tsien, since leaving the United States, has been heard from twice. On Dr. von Kármán's seventy-fifth birthday in 1956 he received the following letter:

"On this occasion of your seventy-fifth birthday, Dr. von Kármán, what would be the proper words for a greeting? Shall I speak about our happy days together in Pasadena, in your house in Pasadena? No, that would not be proper, for I am not just your friend but, more important, your student. Shall I speak about your great contributions to science and engineering, and wish you will do more in the forthcoming years? No, that would be only a restatement of a world-known fact and a repetition of very common birthday greetings. I wish to say more, to say something which may have a deeper meaning—because you are my respected teacher.

"I presume that at the heart of every sincere scientist the thing that counts is an everlasting contribution to the human society. On this point, Dr. von Kármán, you may not feel as proud as you might feel about your contributions to science and technology. Is it not true that so many of the fruits of your work were used and are being used to manufacture the weapons of destruction, and so seldom were they used for the good of the people? But you really need not think so. For, since I returned to my homeland, I have discovered that there is an entirely different world away from that world of the U.S.A. where now live 900 million people, more than a third of the world's population, and where science and technology are actually being used to help for the construction of a happy life. Here everybody works for the common dedicated aim, for they know only by working together can they reach their goal in the shortest possible time. In this world, your work(s), Dr. von Kármán, are treasured, and you are respected as one who through his contributions to science and technology is helping us to achieve a life of comfort, leisure, and beauty. May this statement then be my greeting to you on the occasion of your seventy-fifth birthday."

Upon the death of von Kármán in 1962, Tsien sent a cable to funeral arrangers at Cal Tech from Peking, China:

"I learn with deep regret the passing of Dr. von Kármán, but I believe he, as a brilliant scientist, will live in the hearts of all of us. We can further comfort us by knowing that his scientific contributions will be acknowledged by all countries irrespective of social systems."

All other activities within China unknown to this date; suspect similar research to Cal Tech duties re nuclear and missile development. Agent RM-O-A117, under PROJECT RED MASK, assigned Tsien observation 17 Oct 62. No further word.   END

—Compiler: Lt. James F. Moser
277451 USN
14 Dec 62

* * *

Chang Kwok-wah showered under a stinging jet of icy water and then submerged himself quickly into a hot bath. He languished in the blue-tiled sunken tub, letting the scented water wash away his memory of the incidents yesterday in the Taklamakan Desert. Steam rose lazily, and the mirror over the washbowl began to opaque with condensation. Chang sat back and half-dozed, feeling his muscles relax in relief. He felt drained, and somewhat apprehensive about the reception he would attend tonight.

He lay in the bath for twenty minutes, then stepped out and rubbed himself vigorously with a rough, dry towel. Then he wiped the mirror clear. The tall Chinese looked at his image, and with his slender right hand traced a thin scar which followed his jaw and chin line. It was no wider than a wrinkle on one's palm. He peered intently at his face—at the near-black eyes, set farther apart than normal, at the nose, more prominent than on most Orientals, but his nostrils flared in typical Oriental fashion. His beard was light and required almost no effort to scrape smooth. His lips were thin, and his engaging smile always revealed evenly spaced and obviously well-cared-for teeth.

Chang finished shaving, combed his straight black hair in the official nondescript style, and splashed a highly alcoholic jasmine-scented lotion on his face and neck. Then he dressed for the evening's event.

Outside, he waited patiently for his limousine, and the mellow evening breeze quickly evaporated the alcohol in his cologne, invigorating him.

The reception was being held in the Hall of Supreme Harmony, the largest of the ceremonial halls in the Forbidden City. When he arrived Chang noted the graceful bronze crane, with its serpentine neck stretching skyward. The piece was magnificent, and stood symbolizing strength and longevity. All about the Inner City were ornate and imposing artifacts, temples and scientific institutions built long, long ago when Peking was the center of learning and culture. As he walked up the stairs, he saw the stylized dragons intricately chiseled on the heavy redwood doors, which had been taken from the Buddhist Shrine at Yun-Kang, near the Gobi Desert.

Inside the foyer, government and university official greeters were gathered around a brass celestial sphere mounted on imported Travertine marble, a booty relic plundered from an ancient observatory near Nanchang. At the sight of Chang, several of the greeters bowed deeply and smiled, nodding animatedly. Chang acknowledged them with only a slight bow, and stepped past the heavy sphere into the auditorium.

Various members of the Social Affairs Department, the Scientific Affairs Department, and the Ministry of Economic Well Being were clustered in groups, chatting and drinking *Kaoliang,* a strong vodka-like liquor made from barley stems. A central buffet table was set with detailed care. Gold plates held fresh fish from Canton and even lobsters, normally a rarity in China. There were fresh vegetables from the fertile Red Basin north of Chengking; rice and sweet potatoes from the rocky, rolling hills of Canton. Chang sampled a tidbit and found it delicious.

Under a ceiling segmented by oakwood into thousands of hexagons of color and gilt hung a giant cloth poster. It was a gaudy painting, almost cartoon-like, of Chairman Mao superimposed over an artist's rendering of Chinese youths and military aircraft. Utterly tasteless, Chang thought.

Toasts were made frequently, and most often to the father of the new China society, Chairman Mao, and the culture's new hero, Dr. Tsien Hsue-shen. The language was *Kuo-yu* and the dress was formal. Chang wore his perpetual light blue *Jem-ming,* the quality of which indicated his high stature in the university. He took a small cup of *Kaoliang,* swirled it in his mouth and cringed inwardly as it seared its way to his stomach.

A tall thin man, whom Chang recognized as the Minister of Athletics, saluted Dr. Tsien. "Your magnificent contribution, Dr. Tsien, will give the great Peoples' Republic of China a stronger right fist with which to crush the imperialist aggressors!" The group laughed and sipped more *Kaoliang.*

Another man raised his own cup and chortled, "How ironic that the aggressors themselves have trained your eminent mind to develop this wonderful victory." The man was a student of Tsien.

Chang smiled automatically, and took another drink from the delicate porcelain cup. He thought of Tsien's past—how the genius of this man had been developed at the Massachusetts Institute of Technology on the opposite side of the globe. He thought, too, of the ever-present source of jokes and amused quips that were constantly made about the foolish Immigration Service.

Chang and Tsien had often discussed his past. Tsien felt no remorse whatever in leaving the United States and, in fact, had become acridly bitter toward the American government he had served so well during the dark days of World War II. Now, Dr. Tsien had dedicated himself to developing China's first nuclear weapons and the short- and intermediate-range missiles to carry them. The vast nuclear installations and test sites at Lop Nor had been pushed upward out of the barren sands by the hands of Dr. Tsien Hsue-shen, himself. Now, a new weapon was yet another of his singular achievements.

Chang Kwok-wah's thoughts were broken as his name was called across the circle of officials. "And you, my friend and faithful aide, Mr. Chang," Dr. Tsien was saying proudly, "deserve your share of the glory this day brings to our great nation."

Chang forced another smile and bowed deeply to the older scientist. "Thank you. Your respect and encouragement have been a great inspiration to me."

"May you enjoy your forthcoming reward—many pleasant days at Tsingtao's shining seashores," another man said to Chang. "The bathing there is the best in our nation, and the sun the warmest." The rest of the men grinned in envy as Chang bowed again, thanking the orator.

"Yes," Dr. Tsien called again, "you must enjoy yourself at Tsingtao after your work here. After your flight to Canton tomorrow, I'm sure you will look forward to it."

Chang grinned again. "I can assure you that after I

leave the meeting at Canton and arrive at Tsingtao, you will all vanish from my mind, replaced for two short weeks by the sand and water."

Then the cordiality was rudely broken by an ochre-clad messenger's clamorous entry into the hall. He announced over a too-loud public address system that Lin Piao and K'ang Sheng requested the company of a small list of people to a hastily called meeting at the Ministry of Public Affairs.

Chang Kwok-wah and Dr. Tsien were on that list.

*   *   *

The Ministry of Public Affairs, located at 15 Bow String Alley in Peking, is a four-story sandstone structure with many small windows staring out at the empty streets. Above the worn brick portico a red star, outlined in neon, glowed mistily through the evening fog, which came to the city during the late summer months. Chang had been here before, many times, and hated it. Inside, it was a labyrinth of gloomy hallways painted a pale apple green. Everything was framed with over-stained mahogany and lit by unfrosted bulbs in white reflectors. Most of the windows were stippled glass in which a wire mesh screen had been laminated. There were no carpets on the floor. Instead, a black and brown speckled linoleum material was blotched and scratched by careless waxing.

K'ang Sheng's office was on the top floor in the east wing—the better part of the building. His offices were furnished tastefully, and a rich grass mat covered the floor. The walls, though, were painted apple green.

Upon entering, the first thing Chang noticed was that the unusually intense leer of K'ang Sheng had vanished this evening, replaced by a concerned frown and extraordinary short temper. The aging security director chattered musically to the assembled group. Chang noticed that he and Tsien were the only two present who were not members of the United Front Workers Department.

Then, in a somber and lower-than-usual tone, Sheng began. "Intelligence has been received that has caused the People's Republic of China the gravest concern and alarm. We have received word of a secret agreement of monstrous proportions between the American imperialists and the Russian revisionists—and, we suspect—other powers. They have grown fearful of our nuclear strength. So afraid are they of our steadily growing might, they plan to deal us the first blow. This agreement is referred to by the code name 'Talbott.'

"This information was received only an hour ago through our intelligence monitoring network through *Chosoren* in Japan and Radio *Pyongyang* in North Korea. I have issued a directive to our intelligence agents located throughout the world to discover the details of this agreement and to take suitable action against the instigators of this plan. Even at the cost of their own lives."

K'ang's face grew red as his anger mounted. "No further information has yet been received, but we will force the information from the lips of someone."

Chang had never seen K'ang so angry or so fierce. He couldn't remember when any intelligence received through *Chosoren* had caused such an uproar. Certainly he had heard rumors of "secret agreements" before, but he knew instinctively it had to be of great world importance for K'ang to call such a somber and excited meeting in the midst of a jovial celebration.

"I do not doubt their intentions," K'ang continued, gesticulating wildly. "You are all aware of what they call 'Operation Tonsillectomy'? This is another aggressive plan of the American and Soviet cowards. They have agreed that if any missiles are fired at one nation it is to be believed without a doubt that its origin was not the other. Hence, they will be certain that the People's Republic of China is to blame and will retaliate against us. Now, this new intelligence we've received indicates they have finally agreed to the ultimate murderous act. They will strike us together!"

By now K'ang Sheng's voice was high-pitched in frenzy. His words reverberated throughout the room. "And they will *die* together!"

The words thundered through Chang's mind. "They will die together." They had the fervor and the tenor of idle threats he had heard a thousand times before. And now these words were backed up by an awesome power that could turn planes or missiles to harmless dust, leaving China free to work her nuclear vengeance on the world from behind a new Great Wall.

But could it be true? He had known about "Tonsillectomy," of course. All China had known about it almost as soon as the agreement had been made. But that could have been an intentional leak, made in the hope that the knowledge itself would act as a deterrent. This was different. This—if it should be true—could be the beginning of the last days of the world.

Chang felt helpless. Through the last few years at the university he had been a virtual prisoner of his fame and importance. He was under a surveillance that was designed to safeguard and accommodate his important personage. But it was surveillance, nonetheless. His scheduled vacation at Tsingtao would be his first taste of freedom in years. And perhaps his last.

Chang sighed, and tried to let his mind go clear. He imagined the luxury of the warm Tsingtao beaches, the soothing cool waters. But the disturbing news kept worming back into his consciousness, nipping at the edges of his thought. It was hard to ignore. It was like a sore on the tip of one's tongue.

*　　　*　　　*

The plane that Chang was to take from Peking to Canton was a Russian-built Tupelev TU-114 four-engine aircraft acquired from the Soviets in 1963. Its short range required a stopover for fuel in Wuhan. Dr. Tsien called at Chang above the whine of the turbojets. "Be certain to collect *all* the copies of the technical papers at the conference."

Chang nodded. Tsien had always insisted on giving him the obviously fatherly advice. Chang smiled and watched the older man giving him last-minute instructions. ". . . and be sure to have a closed session with Dr. Tung-chi about his computer delay circuits."

Chang shook his head patiently at the balding scientist.

He smiled at him reassuringly. "I will. I'm most anxious to see what he is doing in that field. Most important, if you'll forgive me, I am also anxious for two weeks of undisturbed pleasure at Tsingtao."

"You deserve it, my friend."

"I'm going to tour the countryside on my way to Tsingtao directly afterward. I will send you all the material from the conference at Canton." Chang thrust a sheaf of papers at Tsien. They were labeled: "Statement of Activity and Itinerary."

Then Chang Kwok-wah bowed respectfully and turned to board the plane. The handsome Chinese felt a momentary sorrow as he stepped inside. He was fond of Tsien and had been treated well by him. Now, he would never see his friend again. Chang sat back in the firm foam-rubber seat. He mechanically fastened his seat belt.

Late last night, in K'ang Sheng's office, the needle of frustration had pierced Chang's membrane of indecision. After the conference in Canton, Chang knew he would try to escape from Red China.

CHAPTER TWO

DEPARTMENT OF DEFENSE
Office of the Secretary of Defense

TO: Admiral of the Navy, Simon Hughes, the Pentagon

Dear Simon:
I'll be sending a special transfer request to your office in a day or two and I'd like you to rush it through as fast as possible.

It's for a Captain James F. Moser, whose serial number I don't have at the moment. Apparently he's one of your brighter young intelligence men, and we'd like to move him over to the Seneca Corp. out on the coast to act as liaison and coordination man for our Advanced Special Weapons Project. As you know, we've been collecting as many "old China hands" as we can and inserting them into key positions in advance of the Talbott date.

Moser will be working specifically on a Project DEI-MOS (for Defense Evaluation and Investigation of Mentally Oriented Systems), in which a Dr. Harrison Haley is getting some fairly interesting results in a psychokinesis study. He's got a young man who can deviate a beam of light merely by concentration, and Haley believes we can eventually put this ability to some strategic use. It's a far-out concept, but one we're highly interested in. Moser seems to be the ideal man, considering his background, previous intelligence work and China experience.

Anyway, the whole Seneca thing is aimed at giving ourselves every possible military advantage by 1972. So I'd appreciate your expediting the transfer when it comes through. Many thanks.

How's your golf game? Didn't have much of a chance to chat at the last meeting, so let's get together one of these "slow weeks" for 18 holes at Burning Tree.

Thanks again.

Regards,

Lawrence Golding
Secretary of Defense

DOSSIER: JAMES FRANCIS MOSER, 277451 USN

DATE OF BIRTH: 6 Nov 26   HEIGHT: 5 ft. 10 in.
PLACE OF BIRTH: San Francisco,   WEIGHT: 169 lbs.
Calif.   HAIR: Brown
MARITAL STATUS: Single   EYES: Blue
NATIONALITY: American, Natural-born

EDUCATION: Good Shepherd Parochial (primary); St. Ignatius High School; University of San Francisco, B.S. Psychology; B.A. Science and Philosophy; ROTC program.

PARENTAL BACKGROUND: Father Kenneth Francis Moser, born Bradenton Beach, Florida; machinist; deceased 16 Oct 61. Mother: Claire McGuiness Moser, born Newport, Rhode Island; seamstress; deceased 2 Apr 63. No other children; Moser—no next of kin.

PHYSICAL CHARACTERISTICS: Chicken pox scars: over right eye, just under left nostril. Childhood scars: two stitches, right cheekbone; four stitches, left kneecap; appendicitis scar; seven stitches, left ankle; two stitches, right elbow. Mole: back, third quadrant; lower abdomen, left side. Heartshaped birthmark, left buttock. Circumcision scar, glans deferens.

COMMENTARY: James F. Moser is stocky; well-muscled frame. No physical abnormalities of serious nature. Athletically active since second year high school; excelled in high school and collegiate sports—swimming, baseball, some boxing. Physical mannerisms are flicking fingernails when nervous; has a tendency to slouch. Dresses well when out of uniform; always neat and well groomed. Dental history good (X rays enclosed), no dentures; hearing: 20/15; eyesight: 20/20; annual physicals indicate general health excellent; no habit-forming indulgences; non-smoker, drinks seldom. Psychological testing: Stanford-Benet: 95th percentile; Missouri-Grant: Stable.

BACKGROUND COMMENTARY: James Francis Moser joined the United States Navy immediately after graduation at age 21. He was assigned to the island of Formosa, 15 Jan 48, as aide to Vice-Admiral Henry R. Steinmetz, head of U.S. team coordinating Generalissimo Chiang-

Kai-shek's National Chinese government organization. Stationed there for over three years, during which time he acquired fluency in five Chinese dialects (Mandarin, Shanghainese, Taiwanese, Cantonese, and Shantungese). Moser has been recognized as United States Navy's foremost authority on China since termination of Formosa assignment. Attached 7th Fleet operating Korean waters 16 Apr 51 Navy Intelligence. He was assigned professorship of PROJECT RED MASK 4 Mar 57 until present. Duties were Philosophy of Oriental Societies; Oriental Psychology; Oriental Customs and Manners; Language Assistant under Prof. Ho Ming-lin.

—Compiler: Lt. (j.g.) Richard N. Devencenzi
445109 USN
29 Mar 69

UPDATED HISTORY: Re-assigned 1 Aug 69 as special coordinator of new Dept. of Defense Project DEIMOS parapsychology study. Orientation tour, SENECA CORP., Santa Monica, Calif. 3 Aug 69.

* * *

Moser's pumpkin-colored Porsche 911 snaked through the sun-reddened Washington, D.C., streets. The windows were down and a soft wind splashed at his face, wafting occasional sweet summer scents through the car. Seven years is a long time; he'd forgotten how balmy evenings could be in Washington. He wound around the interminable and inconvenient circles, remembering now that they were designed by Lafayette to protect the Capitol Building. Such protection was useless, Moser thought, gearing down. They'd burned it anyway.

The sky was ablaze with cumulus clouds that changed imperceptibly from tangerine to pink to magenta, deepening day into evening. Reflections in the chrome ornaments on the car raced in scarlet patterns across his fresh clean uniform. Nice effect, he thought—a good omen for the evening. It had been a long time since he'd attended a full-blown cocktail party. Moser felt a long-forgotten excitement itch at him, and he consciously accelerated toward the fashionable Georgetown section, turning right on "O" Street.

He maneuvered the automobile into an undersized space, locked it, and stood looking at his destination, a three-story brick and mortar building probably built at the turn of the century. This was the home of an old and good friend, Senator William Custer. Moser headed up the walk, admiring the gracious dwelling, remembering it. Seven years. Long time.

The house was meticulously landscaped, Custer's wife Margaret manicuring and detailing the shrubbery and plants with a disciplined regularity and affection. Inside she had redecorated and refurbished it to conform to her taste for traditional and early-American decor. It was a pleasant home, and on warm summer nights the rear double doors would be thrown open and cocktails served on the flagstone, ivy-walled patio. Tonight this area would be lit with green and blue outdoor lights, and Moser knew the Sadwo crystal and Lenox china would be set out in a precise order on an Irish lace cloth. No real glitter, he thought, but a fine patina of quality.

He rang the bell, hearing convivial sounds at that close range. Eli, the Custers' portly butler, opened the door and suddenly Bill Custer was there bear-hugging Moser and erasing years of mutual neglect with the warm and boisterous greeting.

"Well, I'll say you're a hell of a letter-writer, Moser!"

"Yeah? Well, if it's letters you want . . ." and Moser lowered his voice to a privacy-tone, "don't propose any more RED MASK projects! There were lots of do's, but more don'ts!"

The ice was broken, any possible embarrassment removed by the geniality of his host. "If you tell me you've got your guitar in the car, you get thrown out right off." Custer laughed. "What have you been up to, anyway?"

Moser grinned back at him, still clasping the older man's hand. "No, I'm much better on the *wu-chin* now, as a matter of fact. Want me to bring it in?"

"What the hell's that?"

"Chinese. It's that twangy out-of-tune instrument al-

ways playing in the background of Charlie Chan movies.
They use real catgut. Sounds dissonant to you Western
types."

"Never mind," Custer said. "We've got some professional types tonight. Good to see you, Jim!"

Moser nodded and looked around him, eyeing the
scene beyond Custer's shoulder. "Summertime" tinkled
out from the room beyond, contorted into a foxtrot for
the occasion. "I hear 'em," he said. "Properly professional. Good crowd."

"Listen," Custer said, noting Moser's interest, "we
can't get together for a while yet because I've got a little
bargaining to do upstairs before these guys get too stoned.
Go on in and mingle, and by all means have some champagne. We've got Almaden *Blanc des Blancs*—nothing
but the best since our last President's 'America Uber
Alles' pressure!"

"Mingle," Moser said. "Are you nuts? I haven't even
been to one of these things in seven years. What foot do I
start on—and what's champagne? I'm hooked on *Kaoliang.*"

Custer looked at him. "You'll change if you're here
long enough, or maybe our enterprising Chinese friends
will discover a way to carbonate their stuff." As he finished the sentence Custer was already half-trotting toward
the doorway again, waving to Moser as he went.

Moser walked toward the tinkle and chatter, a little uncomfortable, wondering if he'd know anyone, if he'd remember how one made small talk. He paused at the
door, a spectator.

A six-piece combo was grinding out Muzak-type background themes, stilted, over-rehearsed, and pat. Right
now the group was lurching its way through "I'll Get By"
while fifty-odd people strained to converse above the in-
creasing din of the party. Groups clustered here and
there, cradling their champagne glasses, tilting their gold-
rimmed highball tumblers. The handcut crystal twinkled
and the engraved senatorial crest glinted in reply. Moser
stepped in—a participant.

A Negro waiter came by and Moser accepted a glass of

champagne. He sipped, felt the cold effervescence nip at his tongue and tickle his nostrils. A pleasurable discomfort. He rolled the bubbly liquid around his mouth, letting his tongue swim in it, swallowed, and took another sip. Not bad.

On the patio outside, a group of senators soberly and knowledgeably discussed the national debt, while inside, near a Baldwin concert grand piano, a French diplomat argued with two Philippine Army officers about the gold flow. A Marine general, flanked by two impressed subordinates, held forth to a large group in front of a bay window, vehemently stating the case for a stronger military concentration in Vietnam. A smaller covey surrounded a prominent Southern conservative senator who was still stinging from a recent defeat in the matter of a Supreme Court decision.

The combo was well into "Everything's Coming Up Roses" in three-quarter time, and Moser hated waltzes. He mentally began his own arrangement when his vision tunneled down to a tightly-corseted matron who had escaped the Marine general and was now zooming at him from across the room. "I'm dead," he thought, "sunk by a flowered torpedo." The sight of her, along with "Everything's Coming Up Roses" in three-quarter time, seemed to Moser's mind perfectly congruous. He prepared himself with a gulp of champagne and awaited her arrival with stoic resignation. There was no escape. "We who are about to die . . ."

"I just knew as soon as you came in you were that handsome commander Margaret's been talking about," she bubbled.

Moser suppressed a mental groan. "Actually," he said courteously, trying to remain as accommodating as possible, "I'm *only* a captain."

She didn't get it, as Moser knew she wouldn't. "Oh, we'll see about getting you a raise, young man," she giggled. "You know, Bill Custer is quite the string-puller these days."

"Well, I appreciate your efforts, Mrs. ——"

"Anderson," she said, sipping her champagne between information. "Thelma Anderson, Carl's wife."

"Mrs. Anderson," Moser went on, "don't try too hard to get my rank changed."

She nodded at him blankly. "Oh?"

They cat and moused where-are-you-from and what-do-you-do to "Mood Indigo," then swung into hobbies with "Tea for Two." Moser's glass had gone dry, and they were hanging precariously over the Grand Canyon on one of the Andersons' vacations during the slowest rendition of "I've Grown Accustomed to Her Face" that Moser had ever heard. "My God," he thought, "I think it's *our* song."

The rescue was pleasant. It began with Mrs. Thelma Anderson's, Carl's wife's, eyes diverting from Moser's, past his ears, at the precise time he felt the tap of a very gentle, very feminine hand on his epaulet. "Pardon me," said a husky, musical voice. "Are you Captain Moser?" At the word "Captain" the well-meaning older woman excused herself and scooted off in embarrassed confusion before Moser could even offer the farewell amenities. He turned to his deliverer.

A pair of clear turquoise eyes looked frankly into his. An inviting mouth smiled at him—and said words. "I have orders from 'the Boss' to relieve you from that incredible woman."

Moser grinned. "Thanks. She certainly doesn't bore herself. Who's 'the Boss'?"

"Me," she laughed. "I hope you don't mind my butting in."

"Hmm," he said. There were the turquoise eyes under high-arched brows, a fine straight nose, together in that lovely, oval face. He pulled himself together. "Hmm . . . er, no, no I certainly don't mind a bit," he grinned. "What's your name, Boss? I'm Jim Moser."

"Bernadette Talbott."

Moser was surprised. "Are you the gal who wrote that book, *The Brain of a Nation?*"

"*A Nation's Brain*. And I'm flattered."

Moser retained his smile. "Don't be. I didn't like it."

"Have you written a better one?" she asked smugly.

Moser shrugged. "Horse on me."

"I beg your pardon?"

"I just meant you've scored a point. Now I'll shut up about your book. The saying . . . it's a San Francisco thing." Moser continued his examination.

Burnished copper hair curved around her head and swung up against the chin line of the summer-tanned face. She wore a sleeveless white and courageously short silk dress for what Moser had decided was a stuffed-shirt party. The smooth shoulders matched her face, and nicely formed breasts made firm, young-looking scallops through the white silk. Nice waist; good legs, either tanned or in panty-hose. It was a good body, Moser concluded. How old, he wondered? Not super-young; she'd written that book; educated, of course.

He'd already discovered she had a little habit of moistening her lips, and they glistened in the tanned oval face. At times it was hard to tell whether she was smirking or smiling. Her entire expression was one of perpetual anticipation, as if, even when she was talking, she expected an immediate reply.

"I hear you're just in from the Coast," she smiled.

"Being re-assigned."

"Secrets, I suppose."

"Well, I've been re-assigned. This is my first party in quite a while." ·

"Frankly, you could have picked a better one. Where have you been?"

"Can't tell you. May I fill that for you?" He motioned toward the empty highball glass. "It might help a dull party."

"I could get it."

"No, better let me tag along. I think Mrs. Anderson has fallen in love with me."

"I'm sure of it. What are you going to have? More champagne, or something a bit more potent?"

"What are *you* drinking?"

"Scotch. Champagne and I aren't compatible."

"No, champagne is fine. By the way, I apologize for

what I said about your book. It's just that I didn't agree
with some of your conclusions."

"It was written when I was younger. Influenced a little
too much by Ayn Rand, I'm afraid. Anyway, let's not
talk about it. Frankly, the subject bores me now."

Moser sipped his champagne. "I'd really like to pursue
it just a little. Do you really believe a nation behaves like
a person?"

"Yes. We are what we are and we can't change ourselves. We always behave the way we've *been* behaving."

"But people can change."

"Slowly, perhaps. And how many do? Only an ascetic
can really change his behavior patterns. Nobody loves an
ascetic; we are the United States, and we *have* to be
loved."

Moser looked at her smirk-smile. He didn't feel political this evening; he didn't feel literary. He didn't like
"Everything's Coming Up Roses," nor the flowered-tor-
pedo lady. He felt relaxed and a little on his way to being
potted. He wanted Bernadette; and he wanted to leave.
"You said something about this being the wrong party?"

She laughed. "What's the matter? Aren't you having a
good time? You said this was your first party in a long
time. They'll dance later and you could . . ."

He laughed. ". . . dance with the matrons of Old
Fall's Church? Listen, I have to do a little political ma-
neuvering with Bill Custer. Why don't we meet later?"

She looked at him for a long time; at his eyes, the light
brown hair, the chicken-pox scars. Then she smiled that
curious grin. "Brick apartment, corner of Thirty-fourth
and 'Q.' Not far from here. You can remember that, can't
you, Captain?"

He watched her until she vanished among the dark
suits and uniforms and flowered chiffons weaving on the
patio.

*   *   *

At ten-thirty that evening Bernadette Talbott relaxed
over a mild Scotch and water, waiting for Moser to ar-

rive. She was sure he would. She glanced at the clock again and reached for another cigarette.

Bernadette Talbott was born and raised in Boston, Massachusetts. Her early interest was writing, and when she attended Bryn Mawr College in Pennsylvania she was editor of the literary quarterly. However, the influence of an economics and history professor piqued her interest in politics. She decided to attend Yale University for post-graduate studies in International Affairs. Armed with her doctorate and a confident feminine charm, she accepted an assistant professorship at Yale's International Affairs Department. During this time, she met and married William Custer, Jr., a foreign correspondent for *The New York Times*. Bernadette's steady climb to prominence and prestige among the Eastern establishment's intelligentsia was not to be without tragedy. Only six months after their marriage, Senator Custer's son was killed in a plane crash in Europe, and Bernadette found herself a widow, and alone. With Senator Custer's encouragement, she lost herself in her work. The steady stream of brilliantly incisive articles and books buoyed up her reputation until now Bernadette Talbott was considered an unofficial, but influential, member of the past administration's brain trust. It was her 1962 best-selling book, *A Nation's Brain*, that catapulted her to the highest social and political echelon in Washington, and into the First Chair in the International Relations Department at Yale University.

Now, at thirty-six, Bernadette found herself losing interest in the stuffy establishmentarians at Yale. Impatience with the colorless, closed minds of Washington was a frequent experience.

She had been happy in her New Haven apartment during her first appointment at Yale, and chose to stay there even after her promotion, declining the ostentation of the home offered her as a new member of high-ranking faculty. Increasingly, however, she found she was required to be in Washington, and finally took an auxiliary apartment there. As much as possible, she shunned both the academic social calendar and the command performances expected in Washington, making each of her homes serve as refuge from the demands on her time.

Nestling into an arm of the aquamarine sofa, Bernadette thought she had come to like this apartment best of all. Perhaps because of the traffic, the heavier population, it was more of a relief once she had arrived. She had done the decorating herself, painting the walls eggshell, and choosing Mediterranean furniture. It was restful, she concluded, and then too, she painted here. Idly, she judged the seascape supported by an easel in one corner of the room. Fair, she thought. Water was difficult.

Apart from this new impatience and an occasional sense of being fragmented, Bernadette was, in her own way, content. She frequently worked all night without sleep, and handled her many teaching and speaking engagements with a seemingly endless supply of energy. Her active mind propelled her into other projects; there on her desk lay the first draft of a novel, and a completed article on the common market had just today been sent to *Barron's.*

She did, however, find time for discreet socializing. Needed it. Wanted it. Inwardly, she was amused at her father-in-law's perpetual efforts to find her another husband; she was happy enough.

She ground out her cigarette; Moser was at the door.

*   *   *

She stood at the curb, laughing and shaking her head, while he opened the car door for her. "I don't believe it! Where are the mice?"

"What do you mean, mice?"

"The color. It's Cinderella's coach."

"Very funny, Cinderella. Hop in, and I'll prove it's got horses!"

They roared off in the Porsche, the night wind blowing her coppery hair back from the oval face. "Well, where are you taking me in this mustard jar on wheels?" she teased.

He bit. "What do you mean, mustard jar?"

"This teeny tiny car," she chided. "What do you really do, wind it up?"

Moser's consternation grew. "Listen, I just bought this thing when I got re-assigned. I've been driving a heap for seven years and now it's time for some class. And it's got it, baby, so be careful what you say to it. It's one of the finest cars you can own. Great German precision, and all that." He cooled off. "Tuned to real live Wagnerian music, you know. They adjust the accelerator to 'The Ride of the Valkyries.' "

Bernadette laughed again. "Oh, come on. Next to my XK-E this thing looks like something you get for buying a full tank at a gas station." She grinned at him, enjoying his reaction to her needling. She liked him.

Moser's voice rose. "An *XK-E?* Are you crazy? What color is *it*, mauve?"

She kept on. "In this thing you'd never get close enough to find out." The turquoise eyes taunted him.

"Women," Moser moaned, shaking his head. "Don't you know the English are still using paper gaskets? You can't go down the block for a pack of cigarettes without having to re-tune it."

She chuckled. "All right. Horse on me! It's in the shop today!"

Moser relaxed behind the wheel. They drove in silence for a while, each immersed in his own thoughts. Finally, as they neared the Potomac the scent of Daphne perfumed the car, Moser turned to Bernadette. "Do you like music?"

"I don't hear much of it. I listen to the radio, of course, but I'm not a record collector. I get to some concerts, even presidential ones. Does that impress you?"

"Nope. Too bad. It's a great form of expression."

"And you . . . ?"

"I always wanted to become a musician, so I finally bought a scroungy guitar in high school. My dad was a machinist and used to play the violin, of all things. Then one day a lathe got the best of him and he lost three fingers on his left hand . . . and that was that. Still, we always had music in the house. Mom used to fumble her

way around on the piano, and we had one of those old
wind-up Victrolas."

"Where are you from?"

"Mom was from Newport and Dad from Florida. *I* was
raised in San Francisco. You know, I don't even know
where or how they met."

"Where are they now?"

"They're both dead."

Again silence. Bernadette lit another cigarette and
looked at the sharp cutout of Moser's silhouette. He was
handsome, she decided, and she noted with approval how
well his uniform fitted him.

"What about *your* folks?" he asked.

"They're both dead, too, Jim. Actually, I never knew
them well. My father was killed in an automobile accident when I was two. Mom had to go to work and I was
sent to live with her sister. She sent me to the best
schools . . . her husband was an architect . . . but we
never really had much in common. We exchange Christ-
mas cards now, but that's all. I'm pretty much my own
boss, always have been. And this may sound naive . . .
or corny . . . but I've always wanted to *do* something.
You know what I mean?"

Moser nodded. "Is that why you went into politics?"

"Partly. When I started college I had all sorts of elaborate visions of being another Gertrude Stein. But a rose is
not always a rose, and I remember being particularly
upset over the Dien Bien Phu massacre."

"Dien Bien Phu? That was back in fifty-three."

"Yes, I know. But that made me realize that we all
share a responsibility in the state of the world today. I
chose to try to change it. *My* way."

Moser grinned at her last two words. "Oh?" he said.
"What's your solution?"

Bernadette didn't answer him. Instead she was staring
straight ahead. The blue-white mercury brilliance from
the street lights flashed across her face. Moser went on,
"I'm sorry if that sounded wrong. But it *is* a logical question."

"Let's not talk about it. Have you decided where we're going?"

"I think it's up to you. I've been gone too long; the hot spots change. What'll it be?"

"We could go to some place like the *L'Espionage,* or the Blue Mirror. Say, we could drive out to Burning Tree. It's quiet there, or will be tonight. It's nice. I think you'll like it. Besides, I can put it on my account. You must be penniless after wasting your money on this doodlebug."

She was right. Burning Tree was practically devoid of its usual gathering of Washington elite, and Moser noted a better brand of music pouring from the jazz quartet than from the party combo. They ordered, and tried the dance floor for a change of pace. They danced well together, Moser pulling her close as the scent of her perfume excited him. They reordered her Scotch and his Carling's and stayed later and later, listening to the silky notes of the vibraharp. It was past one-thirty as they rode in friendly silence back to Bernadette's apartment. She couldn't remember when she'd enjoyed an evening more; she didn't know or care what time it was, and a warm tremor went through her as Moser groped for, and found, her relaxed hand. He squeezed it affectionately.

Now, in front of her apartment, Moser pulled over and switched off the lights. He turned, just staring at her.

Bernadette asked him in for a last drink. She hoped it sounded casual.

*　　*　　*

She preceded Jim into the dark room. Before switching on the lights, she turned and kissed him hard, but briefly, on the lips. Then she moved away from him and flicked on a lamp. "Sorry," she said. "Maybe I had one Scotch too many, but I've been wanting to do that all night."

"You only beat me to it by half a second. I think *I'm* half-bagged on beer!" he laughed.

"Would you like another? There's some in the refrigerator."

"Sure. Why not?" Moser loosened his tie and plopped down on the sofa. Bernadette went to the refrigerator, transferred the brew from bottle to glass, and came back to the living room, settling next to him, kicking off her shoes and tucking her legs under her. "Still not going to tell me what you've been doing?"

"I've had quite a few crazy assignments with the Navy," he said. "Most of them have been classified, so there's not much I can tell you. A lot of Far East duty. I can speak several Oriental dialects. That's a nice painting," he said, gesturing toward the easel. "You're an artist, too?"

"I love to fool around with it. Working in water is more comfortable for me than oil. I actually sold one once." There was the funny, smirking smile. "It was to my father-in-law."

Moser's eyebrows raised. "Father-in-law? You're separated?"

Bernadette sighed. "No, I'm a widow. I was married to Bill Custer's son. He was killed in Europe six months after we were married. It hit me pretty hard for a while; I started drinking too much. But Bill's dad—my husband was named Bill, too—really helped me. Gave me a job to do to get my mind off it. I took six months and went to Japan and Hong Kong. Suddenly my little tragedy paled when I saw the poverty of those people, the little kids starving. It got to me, gave me something to think about on a larger scale than myself."

Moser sipped at his beer, looking at her over the rim of the glass. She was staring at the painting. "I'll buy one," he said.

"What?" She looked toward him.

"A painting. I told you I've got a brand new apartment out on the Coast. Why not let me buy that one when you're finished? I like it."

"Why, you're most complimentary. And nice, Jim. Really."

Moser reached over and pulled her to him. Then he held her chin, lifted her mouth upward and kissed her. He felt her squirm under his embrace and turn herself into him. Then he began to unzip the back of her dress.

* * *

She was asleep now, and he lay naked beside her. He had no idea what time it was. Moser's hand strayed to her soft body, rested gently on her thigh. Of all the women in his memory, this was the first time that Jim Moser didn't want to leave. Bernadette Talbott. He rolled her staccato name over and over in his mind and watched it tumble like dice thrown across his psyche. Like some pink-faced naval cadet, he found himself infatuated.

The telephone beside the bed breached the night's secrecy with an undignified ring. Bernadette stirred beside him.

"Should I answer it?" he whispered.

"No, let me have it. Best if a man doesn't answer, as they say."

She reached for the receiver and sleepily acknowledged the call. Then she handed it to Moser. He took the cold plastic and pressed it to his ear. The voice of Senator William Custer came over the line.

"Hello, Bill. Caught me!"

"Listen, Jim," Custer began, discreetly ignoring Moser's crack, "there's something up at your headquarters. They phoned the party and asked me to contact you at once. They said it's urgent you phone your code immediately."

Moser nodded to him in the blackness. "Thanks, Bill."

He dialed the number, the numerals spinning back in the little glow of the Princess phone, and a voice answered curtly.

"Moser here."

"Moser, this is Anthony Stephenson. Can you get over here right away?"

"I can be over in forty minutes." He felt reluctance nag at him. "What's the matter?"

"Chang is out." The three words hammered into a mushy recollection that quickly jelled into a hard and painful memory of a friend long gone.

"Chang!" Chang was dead. Killed deep within Red China five years ago.

Stephenson's voice was even. "Chang Kwok-wah."

"I'll be right there." Moser slammed the receiver down. He felt Bernadette's hand on his arm, the length of her body warm against his.

"You have to leave?"

"I'm sorry, but I'll be back."

He looked at her in the dimness, then reached out to cradle her cheek in his hand and kiss her gently on the mouth. Then, without saying a word, he dressed and left.

Bernadette turned her head into the pliant softness of her pillow, and reached over to feel the warmth where Moser had lain. She rolled over onto it, and reveled in the residual aroma of his cologne.

CHAPTER THREE

Four days earlier, the man who was to cause the sudden interruption of Captain Moser's evening came staggering out of Red China's Kwangtung Province, into the teeming Portuguese port of Macao. He had purposely circumvented the Lo Wu border bridge into Great Britain's crown colony of Hong Kong, because he was more afraid of being shot by the British than of being rounded up and returned to the interior by Red Chinese border patrols.

He had seen them, a few years ago, the pitiful but unpitied refugees collected by the British and sent home to certain death. He knew the British had a monstrous choice to make—shoot them now or take them prisoner and send them back to die of shooting or worse. On no other terms could Hong Kong remain a free crown colony. So there they lay, shot down a few precious steps from freedom, their relatives searching tearfully the broken, sad remains of the desperate and the brave. Or there they marched, back to torture and worse, marked as deserters from the proud future of the People's Republic.

Chang couldn't take a chance either way. With only fifty immigrants a day being admitted into free Kowloon, he couldn't take a chance at that well-guarded border.

Instead, he chose Macao, although the last confirmation of his contact here had been made nearly six years ago. Just before he reached the border he carefully hid the dilapidated stolen bicycle which had carried him the interminable miles through the backroads from Canton to a point half a mile from the border. Then he climbed through brush and woods, picking his way cautiously, and furtively creeping through fences, until he could see the old railroad station where ancient freight cars were exchanged, and passengers were made to disembark before the train would be allowed to continue to Macao.

He had waited until dark, and had slinked along the shallow and murky canal wall, not far from the station. The canal sickened him, its filthy water putrid and contaminated with human waste. He had to swim underwater for fifty yards before he dared emerge. Lungs exploding, he had almost been spotted at one point, when a border guard approached the edge of the canal to relieve himself.

He found the address of the contact. It was a squalid Portuguese bar and he was to sit on the floor until the bartender told him to move. Then there would be a code reply and a chance for a safe trip.

But no one came. No one spoke to him, emaciated specimen that he had become. The two days' treacherous exodus from the technical conference at the University of Canton had taken a terrible physical toll. The blue *Jemming* tunic he wore over his blue trousers seemed two sizes too big, when a week ago it had stretched tautly over his muscled chest. His legs ached, his arms trembled, and a cut on his hip throbbed constantly. The years of university work, with special treatment and priority living quarters, had softened him more than he had realized. He looked down at his once-smooth hands, bruised and blistered now. His thumbnail was nearly torn off.

Finally—not the bartender, but someone he took either to be the waiter or the bouncer came over and kicked him sharply. "You want something?" he growled in sloppy Cantonese.

"Where's the bartender?" Chang countered.

"I'm number one man here now," the man replied. "This my place and you drink or get out."

Chang struggled painfully to his feet. His pockets held only worthless Chinese coupons, and he was starving. He hadn't a single Portuguese *pataca* and it was obvious that he couldn't beg for food here. He got to the door and slid down to the ground to think.

No contact. Not even a place to hide. But he was inwardly relieved that no one in this dingy part of town seemed to care about refugees. No one gave him a second glance. But, weak as he was, he still yearned with an inner strength to reach his destination, to talk to the one man he knew could help.

He looked at the broken-windowed clock, and once again at the filth around him. He didn't dare chance a trip to the better part of town, but this slum was beginning to tell on him. To an ordinary Chinese refugee, perhaps, it wouldn't be so oppressive—but he had been one of Peking's elite, respected and admired at the University.

He watched a half-naked baby play with a beer bottle cap, dangerously slipping the sharp and barbed edges of it through his gritty fingers, while, through the doorway, its mother hustled a seaman already drunk on the cheapest whiskey in town.

Chang Kwok-wah tried to think. He had laid his cover as carefully as he could. Still, he couldn't be certain it was perfect. He had made much at the University of looking forward to two full weeks of uninterrupted rest at the Tsingtao resort, and had been especially careful to send Dr. Tsien a proper note explaining again that he, Chang, also planned to see the countryside en route. That, he calculated, would explain credibly his not being at Tsingtao immediately after the conference ended. From there it had been a simple matter to steal a bicycle and head for Macao. In two weeks, however, they would know for sure that he had disappeared.

He had two choices. He could sit around Macao and observe the frenetic preparations for an elaborate funeral about to take place for the late governor. Flower-laden pedicabs, the explosion of firecrackers, and distant drumbeats had already begun the macabre fiesta. He could stay and watch the celebration, trying to keep from being conspicuous, but still running the risk of attracting undue suspicion while he waited. For what? For some sort of contact with the free world? It was a remote possibility now. He would have to sleep where he could in alleys and sidestreets far away from the *Avenida Almeida Ribiro*, hoping to make a contact.

He had to reject the idea immediately. The risk was too great and he had no way of knowing how long he could last without collapsing. A babbling stupor was his primary fear—the things he might say in a delirium.

He settled on the second alternative.

While he still had his drive and while he still had some iota of strength to get about quickly, he had to reach Hong Kong, had to reach the American Consul there. The only ways to get there, he knew, were by air or by ferry—both which were out of the question. Further, he couldn't conceal himself on board any ship because heavy silting in the harbor prevented Macao from being used as an active port.

For Chang Kwok-wah there was only one way into Hong Kong. He would steal a junk and try to get past the British Harbor Patrol without getting himself shot—if he didn't starve to death during the fifty-mile trip in the fragile boat.

* * *

Chang was bleeding profusely from the shoulder. The gash he'd received from the splintered edge of the boat while ducking British bullets was a nasty one. By the time the Water Police boarded the rickety junk, he was unconscious, and the uniformed men peered down at him through their flashlight beams to see if he was still alive.

"Only wounded, dammit!" One of the men knelt beside the bleeding Chinese refugee, estimating the injury. "Well, let's finish him off and be done with it."

The second man gazed down in disgust, and drew his sidearm. "Stand away," he said brusquely. "I'll do him in."

The first man got up and paired with the second to look at the pathetic form on the bottom of the boat. They examined him with their torches. Then the muzzle of the gun entered the beam and followed it, the trigger finger tightening.

"Hold on!" the first officer said suddenly. "Maybe we'd better not."

"Why not? Let's do the bugger in and get on with it."

"Not this one, Stewart. He's someone special, I'll wager."

"This one? Why?"

"He's got that expensive material for a jacket. And they told us not to shoot any of the blue-coated ones. We'd better call him in." The man knelt again beside Chang, feeling the unconscious man's coat. Then he nodded silently, and searched for a pulse.

"Maybe so," the patrolman reluctantly agreed.

"I'm sure of it. Let's get him to a hospital and call the authorities."

The water churned blackly as the patrol boat headed for the shore of Kowloon City, towing the tiny junk. Shouts from the two men brought a battery of British police to the dockside. A lieutenant stepped forward briskly, motioning two officers into the bobbing junk. Perfunctorily, they searched for narcotics.

"Catch us a fish, officer?" the lieutenant inquired.

"Think we might have, sir. He's got a good quality coat—and it's blue. Thought we'd better not chance losing him, though he's wounded as it is."

Orders went out for an ambulance, and the lieutenant went down to make his own examination. "Good you didn't pop him off, all right. That's the right kind of tunic. Good show. I'll advise the Consul."

*   *   *

In Queen Elizabeth Hospital, Chang's wounds were cleaned and probed, then medicated and bound. He slept on throughout his sudsing and bathing. An intravenous contraption was set up, and strength began to drip into the veins of the weakened refugee. Outside the door of the private room a police guard stood his post, and inside, a nurse held vigil through the night.

By morning Chang was conscious and aware of the little white room. The nurse approached him with a professional cheeriness. "Here you are! Feeling better?"

He understood her, and was aware that he had probably escaped, but he simply stared into her eyes.

She shrugged. "Didn't *think* you spoke any English," she said. "Well, I've done my bit. Ta, love. Someone else can have you now." She turned and left the room. Before long, a different nurse entered, accompanied by an intern, who began a routine checkup on pulse, temperature, respiration, blood pressure. Chang drank the fruit juice the nurse offered, but remained silent, acknowledging nothing.

The intern finished. "Well, your condition's not too bad considering how you looked last night. There's someone out there wants to see you. I'll send him in." Chang merely stared.

A moustached man introduced himself, first in English and then in clumsy Mandarin, as Edward Downes from the British Embassy. Chang waited until the man had finished, nodded slowly at him, and asked in a whisper for a piece of paper. Downes fumbled in his coat pockets and came up with a pad and pencil, shoving them at Chang. With a shaky hand, Chang scrawled:

It is urgent that I talk with an official from the American Consul immediately.

Downes frowned at the Chinese. A Red Chinese elite giving me orders, he thought. The ruddy bastards are out to get us all. He nodded curtly to Chang, and still scowling, left the room.

When the American arrived two hours later, Chang felt

an immediate trust in the man. Tall and grey haired, he introduced himself as Walt Forsiak, showing his credentials to the refugee. Chang read the typed details, automatically checking them against Forsiak's appearance. Forsiak looked back at Chang's dark eyes and straight black hair. He noted that his nose was too long for his face.

Chang nodded, and returned the documents. "I am not an ordinary refugee."

Forsiak smiled. "We know that. It was foolish of you to wear that coat during your escape. You could have been spotted."

"That coat saved my life."

"What is your name?" Forsiak produced a pad of paper from his pocket.

"Before I tell you, I wish it understood that you will follow these instructions. Is it agreed?"

"It is agreed. You have my word."

"I wish you to return to your consulate and obtain the necessary papers for my release. My name is Ben Garcia. I am an American agent. You are to contact Captain James F. Moser of the U.S. Navy Intelligence. It is of vital importance and of the highest national security. I will speak to no one but Captain Moser. That is all I can or will say."

CHAPTER FOUR

Captain James F. Moser slipped the Porsche quickly through the gears and raced through the dark Washington streets toward Langley, Virginia. The news he had just heard had jarred his thoughts away from Bernadette. Chang was out. The three words kept repeating themselves with the steady rhythm of a metronome. Moser found it hard to believe. There *had* to be some mistake. Chang was dead. Another CIA snafu?

He walked toward the concrete portico of the CIA, brushing past two slim-legged WAC sergeants who saluted him. He didn't return their salutes but winked genially, causing a replying tinkle of laughter.

Moser jogged up the steps and entered the rotunda. There on the wall was an inscription, chiseled into the marble, announcing to all visitors to the Langley headquarters of the CIA the purpose of this vast superstructure of intelligence:

> And ye shall know the truth
> And the truth shall make you free
>   John VIII, XXXII

It was 4:08 A.M. and the second skeleton shift of workers was leaving the code rooms and offices of the headquarters. Moser had never been inside this new building before. Everyone wore badges. The pairs of feet clicked and scraped across the terrazzo floors of the lobby, walking in seeming disrespect over the yellow-beaked eagle of the CIA seal, imbedded in the tile. In the bowels of the building, grey metal cabinets were being secured with tinny thuds, red OPEN signs had been reversed to LOCKED, and plastic BURN baskets were already being taken outside by security officers for their destruction in the shredder and burner.

Moser walked to the three guards behind a roped barrier. He eyed the flag of the CIA: a lemon-beaked eagle and a six-point compass against an indigo background. He was registered and escorted to the top floor. Fluorescent tubes in the hallway cast blue-white light on the staff of early morning personnel. Within the CIA, a man could have his door painted any color but black, and Mondrianic rectangles were scattered down the aisle. Vibrant greens, gaudy oranges, stark reds, purples, and blues— Moser was reminded of a poorly parodied Disney cartoon.

Then at a door numbered 75706 and marked with the

initials "DCI" Moser was escorted into the office of Anthony G. Stephenson, the Director of Central Intelligence. Stephenson's door was white.

Moser had started to knock, but the Marine escort opened the door before he could. "Go right in," he said. "Mr. Stephenson will be with you shortly." The door closed, and the escort was gone.

"Captain Moser, how do you do?" Moser turned, feeling a sophomoric anxiety, vaguely as if he'd been called to the principal's office.

Anthony G. Stephenson was the new director of the CIA, and until now had only been a name neatly embossed on letterheads. He was the heretofore unseen superintendent, the invisible commander of the nation's clandestine operation. Moser saw a partially balding man; his hair, or what was left of it, was wispy and uncombed. Behind small steel-rimmed glasses, the reddened eyes were intense. Moser knew that those eyes had already completely absorbed him and, even now, were sending miniscule electric impulses to Stephenson's computer-like brain. Stephenson did not smile, but thrust a chunky hand toward Moser.

"Captain Moser," he began, forgetting formalities, "come on into my office. There's something I want you to read first."

Moser followed him into an inner room. A pall of anxiety hung in the air like an electric net. The office was austere, simple, nondescript. The walls were paneled in some dark wood, probably mahogany, and hung with some photographs of what Moser assumed were of Stephenson's family and friends. A print of Wyeth's "Christina's World" was framed almost too elaborately. Behind the desk was a portrait of John Robert Burgess, the newly elected President of the United States. The paneling was broken by three long windows overlooking the parking lot and the Virginia hills, which blocked the view of Washington and the Potomac. Behind Stephenson's desk, a bank of colored telephones sat silently on a mahogany filing cabinet, each color having its function. Internal. Ordinary. A direct line to the White House. Another to the

Pentagon. The blue telephone was a direct connection to the President.

Flanking Stephenson's desk were the Stars and Stripes and the omnipresent flag of the CIA, with its grimacing eagle.

Stephenson sat behind the desk and fiddled with his pipe. Then he reached into a drawer and removed a bright green envelope. He slid it across the desk toward Moser, the grating sound it made punctuating Stephenson's somber expression. "Sit down, Captain, and read this. I'll be back in a few minutes."

Moser nodded and picked up the envelope. Stephenson rose and angled his way around the desk. The door closed and the man was gone. Quiet descended on Moser and he unfastened the heavy envelope. Fuchsia block letters on the front of it read:

CRYPTO CLEARANCE
NOT TO BE REMOVED FROM D.O.D.
RED MASK FILE

He noticed the entire file had been recently decoded, and wondered whether it was expressly for his eyes. He glanced around the room, somehow expecting a pair of eyes to be watching him, registering his reactions and movements; but all he saw was the suspended streak of blue-grey smoke that represented Stephenson's wake.

He pulled a sheaf of yellow reports from the green envelope. The front page of the topmost sheaf read:

DOSSIER: GARCIA, BENIAMINO JESUS

and below the legend was scrawled:

Believed killed, Peking or Moscow, 1964

Moser felt a slight pressure in his stomach. He thought briefly of the flu, of nausea, of days when offices such as this one were peopled by deans, commanding officers, grim-faced Formosan officers, South Korean diplomats,

and Laotian dignitaries. These were the offices of the big
wheels, Moser thought. And then he thought of Bernadette and the ensuing incredible phone call. It brought him
back to the present. He read:

DATE OF BIRTH: 18 May 29   HEIGHT: 5 ft. 11½ in.
PLACE OF BIRTH: Chula Vista, WEIGHT: 165 lbs.
Calif.   HAIR: Black
MARITAL STATUS: Single   EYES: Dark Brown
NATIONALITY: American,
Natural-born

EDUCATION: San Gregorio Parochial (primary); Chula
Vista High School; University of Southern California;
BS, Engineering, Physics.

PARENTAL BACKGROUND: Father: Julio Ramirez Garcia, born Ensenada, Mexico, B.C., 1909, dishwasher/
laborer. Now owns small Mexican roadside stand in San
Diego, California. Brief history when younger of Pancho
Villa activity, but no known political involvement as
adult. Two brothers, Ramon and Pedro, both merchants
in Ensenada, Mexico, B.C. Mother: Anna Minelli, born
Genoa, Italy, 1910. Entered USA with parents 1925 via
Nogales, Mexico, from Genoa, Italy. Married Julio Garcia
1930 when Beniamino Garcia was one year old. No
known political activities in Italy. Worked in dress shop
briefly in San Diego, then for husband until her death in
1951.

PHYSICAL CHARACTERISTICS: Childhood scars: 18
stitches, right calf. 7 stitches, right front quadrant of cra-
nium. Mole under left ear. No birthmarks.

COMMENTARY: Beniamino Jesus Garcia is tall, well-
muscled and extremely agile. High school athletics were
football and baseball; college activity baseball exclusively.
Was invited to try out for position in Los Angeles Dodgers
Baseball Club farm system but turned down offer in deference to furthering education and earning Baccalaureate
honors. No physical abnormalities. No physical mannerisms but for slight tendency to over-gesture with hands
during conversation. Posture, dress, excellent. Dental his-

tory (X rays enclosed): more than average childhood cavities; tobacco stains on incisors and canines; missing teeth, T-18 and 19, B-3 and 7. Hearing: 20/20; eyesight: 20/25; annual physicals during training for Project RED MASK indicate excellent perennial health; moderate smoker, moderate drinker. Psychological testing: Stanford-Benet, 97th percentile; Missouri-Grant: Stable.

BACKGROUND COMMENTARY: Beniamino Jesus Garcia was 4.0 student at University of Southern California when he petitioned immediately prior to graduation for USAF intelligence work, 14 Apr 51. Exhaustive testing showed extraordinary ability to learn and perfect languages and scientific concepts. Was subsequently inducted into G-2, 6 Dec 51. Transferred to Pentagon 15 Nov 54 as M/Sgt. in cryptography, serving to 10 May 56. Conference with subject and further psychological and mental stability testing showed ideal subject for Project RED MASK (begun New Mexico, 1948). Subject enlisted immediately after extensive indoctrination; given several opportunities to cancel program but stayed positive and eager throughout processing.

NOTE: SPECIAL INSERTION. NAMESAKE LOCATED 5 Jan 62. NAMESAKE GRADUATED ENGINEERING DEPT. MASSACHUSETTS INSTITUTE OF TECHNOLOGY 1951, AND CONSIDERING POST OF GRADUATE-ASSISTANT, M.I.T., AT TIME OF CONTACT. REMUNERATION OF $45,000 CANADIAN DOLLARS AND LIFETIME PENSION ACCEPTED 12 Feb 62. NAMESAKE COMMITTED TO LIFETIME GOVERNMENT SURVEILLANCE. SUBJECT ACCEPTED POST OF GRAD. ASST., M.I.T. 15 Jun 62 IN TIME SUMMER SESSION. NAMESAKE, RENAMED STANLEY WONG, DRAFTSMAN FOR LOCK MANUFACTURING CO., VANCOUVER, B.C. SEE FILE #40669 FOR SURVEILLANCE REPORTS. END SPECIAL INSERTION.

Cover for Beniamino Garcia laid 17 Mar 57. Check one year later by Lt. James F. Moser, 277451 USN, showed father programmed well, Garcia covered perfectly. Lt. Moser given charge of Garcia upon entrance at Little Shanghai in New Mexico, and stayed in constant personal contact until beginning Project RED MASK.

Without looking up from the dossier, Moser closed his eyes briefly and thought back to 1957. As a young lieutenant coming from Korea, and eager to begin his new assignment at the government's experimental training center in New Mexico, Moser had been momentarily disappointed with the broad, barren deserts. Now, the arid, cactus-speckled scenery flashed before him, and he thought, too, of landing in Santa Fe that bright afternoon. He and the young Mexican boy had laughed en route to the villages—both young, both dedicated and zealous, they had joked about beginning espionage work where no spies could conceivably have been operating. But their humor was short-lived. When they entered what soon became known as "Little Shanghai," the two men stepped into the interior of the Red Chinese mainland.

Moser swallowed and began reading the dossier again, trying to suppress the heavy feeling in his throat.

Garcia assigned as trainee Project RED MASK immediately, attached to Lt. Moser and began identity transference. Medical treatments began 17 Jun 57, with no physical changes until following year. Garcia contacted no one except Chinese agents until Project RED MASK undertaken. At that time Garcia's physical changes were complete and subject fully trained. Beniamino Garcia officially Chang Kwok-wah 17 May 62.

Chang accepted M.I.T. Grad-Asst. post for summer session 24 Jun 62. Red Chinese contact made almost immediately via United Front Workers Dept.

Moser blinked at the beacon-like words. The United Front Workers Department provided the facade for the Red Chinese government. Abroad, it was the link to the 15 million Chinese who are residents of foreign countries. Through this link the UFWD attempts to align overseas nationals in support of the Peking regime and its political activities. Its total function is to encourage defections to the Chinese mainland. Moser recalled one of the UFWD's greatest victories: the defection of Li Tsung-jen, former vice-president of Nationalist China under Chiang Kai-shek. He recalled a second, perhaps more trenchant victory: Dr. Tsien Hsue-shen, a prominent nuclear scientist and rocket expert at the California Institute of Technology's Jet Propulsion Laboratory in Pasadena, had defected after some rather shabby treatment by immigration authorities and overzealous senatorial committees. Under the direction of Tsou Ta P'eng, the UFWD's new theme was "cities will fall when the countryside is mobilized." Those bastards aren't doing a bad job either, Moser thought as he momentarily considered Asia, Africa, and Latin America.

He brought himself back again and continued reading:

Chang kept running contact with Red Chinese agents headquartered at Hsinhua, the news bureau for the New China News Agency (NCNA). Chang defected to Red China 13 Oct 62 through new Cuban channel. Believed to have succeeded in contact with Dr. Tsien Hsue-shen at University of Peking government laboratories and initiated into nuclear research under his direction.

Prior to defection, twelve random security verifications carried out in six cities (New York, San Francisco, Washington, London, Taipei, and Hong Kong). All rechecked by Lt. Commander James F. Moser. Two planned episodes with Hong Kong and Taipei agents both resulted in attempts on Chang's life by U.S. agents in those cities, who are both Chinese Nationalists. Chang also sent for one week to San Diego, Calif.: he was allowed to contact and converse with his own father without identifying himself. Agent on surveillance gave 100 per cent perfect activity report. One minor discrepancy: Chang experienced mental remorse at not being able to effect family farewell.

Chang Kwok-wah became Project RED MASK's official first subject upon China entry. Last contact was in

Peking by Lin Tse-ten, (Agent Gary M. Davis A11603) directly to CAPRICORN, 6 Sep 64.
Message read:
EXPECT NUCBLAST VICINITY LOP NOR PLUS MEG MONTH.
—Compiler: Lt. (j.g.) Thomas C. McDermott
782746 USN
Further attempts at contact have failed.

Moser carefully read the last sentence again, and then stared for a long while at the hastily scrawled updating below the last line:

11 Aug 69

That was two days ago. Moser swallowed hard and wished Stephenson would return.

*   *   *

At nine-thirty in the morning of March 20, 1957, young Lieutenant James Moser landed at Santa Fe Airport, and immediately had misgivings about his new assignment. The quaint, Spanish-styled town was a new-world survivor of the Iberian influences of more than a century ago. Santa Fe was surrounded by the sizzling sands of the desert, whose shimmering heat waves made the distant Sangre de Cristo Mountains quiver and undulate in the hot purple haze.

Moser mumbled to himself. "Whoever in hell picked this place ought to have his goddamn head examined. Christ, I'll bet there isn't even a good Chinese restaurant here." The torch of a sudden blast of desert air hit him as he walked across the ramp.

At the terminal gate, a black air-conditioned Chrysler Imperial, with a black curtain drawn over the rear windows, drew up quietly. It looked very much like a hearse. As Moser waited, a Chinese man behind the wheel beckoned to him. "Lieutenant Moser?"

Moser turned toward the voice, his training telling him not to react. No one could know his rank, he thought, unless he'd been alerted to his description. The light blue and sharply pressed seersucker suit he wore disguised any profession—any occupation. He could have been a doctor or a midwestern cosmetic salesman. His eyes swept past the black car and continued toward the other side of the terminal.

"Lieutenant Moser!" The voice came again as the limousine pulled closer to the curbside.

Moser finally acknowledged the voice. "Right," he said curtly. "Mr. Tan?"

A hand stretched from the open window. "May I see your orders?"

Moser pulled a small packet from his jacket and handed the man a neatly folded piece of legal-sized paper. It disappeared into the car as he waited.

Then the Chinese said, "If you'll climb in the back we can get on our way."

Moser hefted his bulky bag in front of him, wincing as the hot plastic handle hurt his palm. He got in quickly and was surprised to see a handsome Mexican youth in the rear seat. The boy wore a brown flannel suit and Moser noted it seemed too large for him.

"Ben Garcia, this is Lieutenant Jim Moser," the driver introduced them. Moser shook his hand.

"Lieutenant Moser," the driver continued, "you'll be assigned to Garcia for the duration. I'm history and philosophy, so we'll have to have a few get-togethers ourselves."

"Have you been here long?" Moser asked the Mexican boy.

"Couple of days," Garcia said, smiling. "It's sure been hot."

Moser returned the smile. "It's no San Francisco."

"I've never been there," Garcia said. "Or anywhere north of Santa Barbara, really. Can you believe that?"

"I've heard you're from L.A.," Moser kidded, "so I'll believe anything."

The Mexican youth laughed deeply and pleasantly. A good laugh, Moser noted. They chatted amiably about their respective hometowns as the car glided along the asphalt waves for more than an hour. Nothing passed out-

side but ochre desert. Cactus lined the one-lane road, and
the air-conditioner whooshed a steady stream of frosty air
around the passengers. Outside, it seemed as though
nothing lived. The distant mountains of Sangre de Cristo
remained still and passive. Far away.

Finally they drew up to a large cyclone fence where a
sweat-soaked guard checked their ID's. Moser looked
around and remarked to himself that the fence seemed to
enclose nothing but more desert. The fence seemed incongruous. After another short ride, he noticed a pinkish rec-
tangle in the distance, which grew steadily larger. It then
transformed itself into an enormous white billboard on
which were scrawled, as if by vandals, a red-painted series of Chinese characters.

As they neared the billboard, Ben Garcia pointed at it
and asked, "I wonder what that means."

Peering at the board, Moser felt an icicle prick the
back of his mind—the part where Oriental memories lay.
"It's in Mandarin, Ben," he said slowly. "It says, 'Either
the East wind prevails over the West wind, or the West
wind prevails over the East wind. I believe it is character-
istic of the situation today that the East wind is prevailing
over the West wind.' "

"That's an eerie little aphorism, isn't it?" Garcia said.
"Who thought that up?"

Moser looked at him and a sardonic smile creased his
tanned face. "Mao Tse-tung, baby. Your next boss."

*   *   *

They were in Little Shanghai.

The guide talked incessantly, in dreary monotones, as
Moser and Garcia were given their orientation tours. The
two young men were amazed—virtually flabbergasted at
the colossal scope of the secret government settlement.
Little Shanghai was situated in a broad valley somewhere
in the Sangre de Cristo Mountains, and its center was a
vast man-made lake, seventy-two square miles, around
which were sprinkled fishing villages, small seaport towns,
and other shoreline settlements peculiar to mainland
China.

The population was almost exclusively Chinese, numbering more than 78,000 peasants, merchants, bankers, traders, and even political figures, such as mayors and soldiers.

Moser was aghast at the reality of it all. The lake was thronged with junks and medium-sized fishing boats of all types. At one point, in a tiny village where they cruised along the main street, they were stared at—Occidentals in an Oriental town. Moser asked the guide to explain the origin of the locale.

"They're Chinese-Americans," he said through an interpreter. Garcia was hanging on every word, although he spoke no Chinese. "After the retreat of Chang Kai-shek to Formosa, the government made an offer to selected refugees and most of them accepted it. Here the Chinese people in this country can have their own society, their own way of life as they knew it in their homeland. It's as much like their heritage as if they had never left China. They've actually welcomed the chance to begin anew, so to speak—to live a life in the manner they're used to, with the people they prefer and the religions they choose to pursue. The government made this lake, designed the entire colony to resemble in the smallest detail its prototype town in China, and the inhabitants have brought it along themselves quite nicely. They've got businesses, recreations, newspapers—everything they had in China. It's even self-sustaining as far as costs go. They grow their own food, trade among themselves, and the commodities they can't produce are supplied by a government facility that's been set up as a sort of import-export center—just as if their local governments here had decided to ship in, say, rice bowls. Naturally, they've agreed never to return to urban life, and in fact, they're actually voluntary prisoners. They aren't allowed outside, and no one outside knows they're inside. They have no knowledge of Project RED MASK, either. They think they're part of a vast reservation, much like the Indians have. Of course, they're treated much better than most Indians are, sad to say. So that's why there is no English spoken at all on the site. The students will either learn Chinese, and learn the Oriental way of life to the nth degree, or else they'll be reassigned to some other intelligence group."

The interpreter realized he may have become long-winded, and cut himself off. He pulled the car up to a wharf near the shoreline. "Care to get out and walk around?" he asked. "You've got all the freedom of movement you want."

Moser and Garcia demurred, still incredulous at the outstanding size and detailed complexity of the installation. Outside, merchants and peasants alike stared at them, genuinely curious about the car with the Western-garbed men inside. Moser saw no other vehicles, save bicycles.

At the other end of the lake, Moser's and Garcia's awe was doubled by the sight of a compact seaport city, crowded with merchants and workers, fishermen and businessmen. "Jesus," Moser whispered to Garcia. "That's Amoy, I'd swear it." Garcia gaped out the window as the car drew down a long street.

Moser saw a newspaper lying on the ground and halted the car as he glanced at the headline. The large Chinese characters read, to Moser's amazement:

DOUBLE MURDER SUSPECTS SOUGHT

Moser couldn't believe it. "Hey," he called to the guide, "is that newspaper for real? That one said something about a double murder."

"Oh certainly," the guide said. "We've got crime just as any crowded city does. There's even a small prison being built to the north. Everything's quite normal, as you'll see. It should take you a while to get used to it, gentlemen, but for all practical purposes, you are no longer in the United States. You are living in mainland China."

*   *   *

For the next five years, Ben Garcia gradually became Chang Kwok-wah both physically and mentally. He picked up the local dialects quickly, more out of necessity at first than for a formal education. Since no English was spoken, he and his fellow students followed a strict daily regimen, with only a few hours a day reserved for their personal pursuits. They were allowed to comingle with the locals, even date some of the prettier Chinese girls around the lake, but their primary efforts were those of learning all they could, of becoming in every distinguishable way Chinese citizens.

Ben Garcia, now Chang Kwok-wah, studied physics, geography and other physical sciences in the mornings. His afternoons were taken up with the humanities and the arts of China, and his meals were taken seven days a week at a nearby Chinese household. He saw Moser every day, both in and out of classes, and they frequently sailed together on the lake during precious leisure moments.

Five years were spent this way. Inside the Red Chinese mainland. They never left Little Shanghai. Except once.

Moser would remember the sequence of events for the rest of his life. He would remember it with a mixture of pain and understanding; the emotional vortex of disgust and loyalty.

It happened on a warm May evening. Chang had left the Great Institute of Artistic Achievement early for a date with a girl he had been seeing for three months. Her name was Lin Chu-sheng and she was the pretty daughter of a policeman. He was thinking of her as he walked along, unmindful of the odors of the fish-laden avenues that had been so unpleasant when he first arrived. As he crossed a crowded street and passed a darkened and empty alleyway en route to the theater where they were to meet, three men, clad in dark clothes, interrupted him.

They seized his arms immediately and one man covered his mouth with an oily rag. He was dragged into the alley where one of the men beat him as the others stood back watching. One man held his arms.

When he awoke the next morning, he found himself in a bare, musky cell with nothing but a long piece of plywood arranged, ludicrously, as a bed in one corner. The interrogator told Chang he was to sign a confession that

he was actually a Communist, an agent working for the
Red Chinese to infiltrate Little Shanghai and bring back
detailed intelligence information of the secret project
known as RED MASK. Chang, of course, refused, but his
dilemma was a mental anguish.

At first he had thought it all some necessary training
procedure designed to acclimate him in a brutal simula-
tion of what he might expect were he to be captured in
Red China after receiving his ultimate assignment. But
the facts rose harshly to the forefront of his mind in the
swiftly moving first days of his imprisonment. Were they,
in fact, Chinese agents with their own little organization
within Little Shanghai?

For three months he was kept in isolation, questioned
daily and harassed to sign his confession of guilt. He was
forced to live with his own excrement and was starved almost to the point of death. He was beaten frequently with
bamboo whips and on several occasions his testes were
rapped harshly with rubber rods as he stood, agonizingly,
in chains binding him to his stone cell wall.

At one point he was degraded beyond human imagina-
tion; made a veritable animal as he groveled for morsels
of food, all the time begging for mercy but unyielding in
his refusal to sign any document whatsoever. He was forced
to stand in front of a harsh, blazing light that blinded
him. He was stripped naked in front of jeering Chinese
females, also nude, who taunted and mocked him as they
laughed amid their grotesque examinations.

Chang was also forced to eat the vilest of foods, the
bitterest of squid soup in which floated the mushy eyes
and tentacles, whole. Chang ate it. Eyes, tentacles, and
all.

Still, he refused to confess.

Chang's dedication was proved beyond doubt when
one day he was gently led from his cell and brought to a
hospital, where he was treated, bathed and fed a warm,
wholesome meal. He was then apprised of the grizzly les-
son, the severe acclimitization of what it would be like
were he ever imprisoned behind the Bamboo Curtain. He
was then offered the option of resigning from the pro-

gram, of leaving Project RED MASK and being reassigned in U.S. Intelligence work.

Chang, once again, refused.

Moser, in fact, was the more resentful of the two. The details which Chang revealed to him during their three-week rest and recreation leave in Mexico were shocking and Moser experienced deep doubts about the project. They had gone a bit too far, he insisted, but Chang avoided criticism of his ugly ordeal.

It was then, after catching a sailfish, off the coast of Punta Palmilla on the southern tip of Baja California, that Lieutenant Jim Moser first realized that he was no longer a close friend of Ben Garcia.

He was now the closest friend Chang Kwok-wah had in the world.

*   *   *

11 Aug 69

The scrawled updating on the dossier's last yellow page once again jolted Moser back to the present. He dropped the green envelope on the table as Stephenson, a now-unlit pipe clenched between his lips, returned to the office.

"Well, what do you think, Captain?" Stephenson asked almost too casually as he sat down in his chair.

"Hard to believe that after five years Chang finally managed to get out."

"Indeed, it is," Stephenson said. "But we do have someone named Chang Kwok-wah, and he insists on talking to no one but you. I realize you haven't done much work for me directly, Captain, but we're in a bit of a fix here. Which is why we called you."

Moser rubbed his hands. "Chang and I were very good friends. I'm guessing he wants to see me to insure he's not . . . intercepted, or something, before he gets to tell us whatever it is he wants to tell us."

"Precisely. But that's not all."

"But I haven't seen him since Little Shanghai. I'm not sure he'll even recognize *me*, after all."

"That's not what I meant." Stephenson began searching his pockets for a match again. "Naturally, we all realize that everyone's playing the same game. In short, Captain, we want you to verify for us that this is indeed the real Chang Kwok-wah. He fits the physical characteristics, and even his dental X rays have been verified, but we have to admit to ourselves that whatever job *we* can do, the enemy can do *also*."

Moser nodded. "You want me to ask him some personal things, some questions that only the real Chang could answer correctly."

Stephenson then stood up and pushed a button on the wall behind him. "Well, let's get on with it, then."

A moment later there was a knock at the outer door, and Stephenson crossed the room as an armed Marine escorted a handsome Chinese, dressed in olive drab Army fatigues and white sneakers. There were dark outlines on his sleeves where two chevrons were once sewn. Cloth patches on his breast read "US ARMY" and "HARRINGTON." There was a bandage on his right thumb.

The Marine stepped aside and Chang entered the room, closing the door behind him. Then Stephenson approached him. "Mr. Chang," he said.

Chang nodded, looking past Stephenson toward Jim Moser.

Stephenson caught the glance and turned to Moser. "You know Captain Moser here, don't you?"

Moser couldn't move. Chang looked at him for a long moment, and Moser returned his gaze. He saw the pools of memory churning behind mahogany eyes, and Chang's lips remained still as he looked at his friend.

Then Chang spoke. "Which wind is prevailing, Jim?" The Chinese grinned.

Moser, too, broke out in a wide smile as he approached Chang quickly. "Chang," he said simply, and without embarrassment clutched the taller man by the shoulders. Chang and Moser embraced each other for a long moment, until Stephenson coughed self-consciously.

"You gave us quite a scare for a while there, ol' buddy. We thought they'd found you out."

Chang, still smiling, remained stolid. "Impossible for

me to get anything more out. Tsien took a liking to me and I was virtually barricaded from outside contacts. Been working with him night and day for five years now."

Stephenson assumed his professional airs as he motioned everyone to be seated. "Mr. Chang," he said directly, "I'm sure you realize there are some preliminary questions we should ask you."

Chang sat down. "Jim can ask me anything."

Moser felt a bit uncomfortable, but when Stephenson nodded to him, he cleared his throat and looked at Chang. "Well, Chang, I've got to ask you something."

"Go right ahead, Jim."

"Okay. I think two questions will do it. Remember that newspaper I noticed on the street when we first got to Little Shanghai and we were getting our orientation tour?"

Chang frowned. "Newspaper?" he said.

"There was a headline on it that I read out loud. Remember what it was about?"

The room was silent as Chang looked up at the ceiling. Stephenson looked at Chang intently, and Moser made vague motions of coercion with his hands.

"I don't remember it, Jim." Chang was shaking his head.

Moser broke in again. "It was about a crime. Remember the guide told us about a new prison when I asked him about the headline?"

Chang continued to shake his head. "I vaguely remember something about the prison, but I can't recall any newspaper. I'd only be guessing, and that wouldn't do either of us any good."

Moser looked at Stephenson, then back at Chang. "Let me try another. How did we ask the chef at the Los Ramos ranch to prepare the marlin you caught during our R-and-R in Punta Palmilla?"

Chang's face lit up. "You know damn well that we gave the *sailfish* to the local orphanage. But you get one out of three right yourself—we *did* stay at the Hotel Palmilla that evening."

It was Moser's turn to beam as he looked again at Stephenson. "No other person in the world could know that," he said, "but Ben Garcia."

Stephenson then returned his gaze to the Oriental agent. "Chang, I know it's been rough and I know you're tired, but we must have a briefing session immediately. What is this all about?"

Chang sat back and crossed his legs. "I had to escape and lay cover. I couldn't take the chance on waiting any longer."

"But why?" Stephenson was fondling a silver letter opener.

"China has developed some spectacular break-throughs that I have been a part of. These, I can discuss in detail later. Most important, I heard from the lips of K'ang Sheng, the head of Chinese Intelligence, information concerning a most serious security breach from the United States. This information shook the entire arm of the Social Affairs Department to its roots. I was stunned when I heard what the Chinese had found out."

Moser listened intently as Chang spoke quietly with a slight, hesitating, Mandarin accent. Stephenson's eyes were riveted on the refugee.

"The secret is out, gentlemen," Chang Kwok-wah paused. "The secret that you call the 'Talbott Agreement.'"

Moser's own shock at hearing the familiar name passed quickly when he saw the expression on Stephenson's face. The man was transfixed.

"That's impossible," Stephenson said, and added automatically, "there is no such 'secret,' as you call it."

Chang looked at him expressionlessly. "Then how do I have the name, if even *I* am supposed to be in the dark?"

Stephenson seemed to acquiesce; Moser was fascinated. "They know something about this 'agreement'?"

"That's the real reason I came out," Chang said sternly. "Not only do they know about it, but I'm here to tell you that it will fail. The Chinese have developed a defensive weapon that transcends physical science."

Then Chang stood up, as if to leave, but only to emphasize his next point. "It is being assumed that this agreement is some sort of aggressive military plan between the United States and Russia. To state it simply, I escaped to convince you that Red China's defense capabilities, of which you know nothing, are very sophisticated. Such a plan will fail, and that failure could destroy half the world."

CHAPTER FIVE

On Walker's Cay, a small sequestered island in the Bahamas, there is a hidden tree-rimmed villa often used by high U.S. government officials as a meeting place. Most particularly, it is used by member countries of the Alliance for Progress as a half-way point between the Americas. Difficult to find, except by the most knowledgeable navigators in the area, the island is reached only by launch or by seaplane.

Moser had caught the first Eastern Airlines' commercial flight to Miami from Washington, D.C., and knew he'd be early. He stepped off the specially ordered seaplane from Miami and felt the warm tropical breeze on his face. It was early morning, and the sun was boldly splashing the surfaces of island and sea with thick strokes of color. Moser walked slowly toward the archway marking the entrance to the villa. Palms and sand dunes melded delicately into a postcard panorama. The sea was calm crystal reflecting the perfect blue sky. Now and then Moser could hear a bird call, not unlike African sounds on a movie sound track. It was difficult to pinpoint exactly where one was situated on the globe, and harder to believe that in this idyllic spot men talked about wars and bombs, gold and bullets.

Moser reached the arch and crunched along the pebbled path, finally hopping briskly up the wooden steps.

Inside, he was greeted by a Jamaican steward who escorted him upstairs to his room. It was large and comfortable with an unbelievable tropic view from his windows. He felt an ache shoot through him—the kind of ache that whispered, "Don't you wish you were on vacation—don't you wish you could stay?" That's a useless wish, he thought, and began to undress.

He showered and doused himself with cologne to offset the heat. Then he changed shirts and dabbed at the lint on his uniform with one of those sticky gadgets that moved more lint than it removed. He checked his watch; only ten. He adjusted his tie, drank a tall glass of ice water, and went out.

The steps creaked under his polished black shoes as he trotted down into the foyer. "Where will the meeting be held?" he asked the steward. The servant gestured toward double doors, thrown open, and flanked by two U.S. Marines. They saluted, and a third examined his credentials and briefcase, ultimately letting him into the large, air-conditioned parlor.

It was decorated with exotic greenery, expensive rattan furniture, and petrified wood tables. Overhead hung a net with conch shells and starfish dangling from it, and a long-ossified squid lay high on the net in one corner of the room. The walls were plastered with old maps and relics of Caribbean pirate days. Caged in a corner was a brightly colored cockatoo, his green and orange head festooned with a vermillion comb. It squawked and sidled along its perch making little gurgling noises.

Moser immediately noticed the room's only incongruity. On the far wall was a large Mercator projection of Red China, flanked by smaller maps of the world, Russia, and each hemisphere. A chart to one side listed, in crisp black letters, the names of several nations. Under a column heading marked "MILITARY STRENGTH, 1972" was a diverse array of mathematical symbols. An IBM printout sheet near the corner, taped to two wooden voodoo masks, told of air power, nuclear deployment, positions of stationed Polaris submarines, and *Kresta-* and *Kynda-*

class Soviet destroyers carrying the new SS-M-2 and *Styx* missiles.

Another sheet particularly interested Moser. He noticed that the Soviet's Baltic fleet had been X'd out, and replaced with the letters "ASIAN FLEET." He saw, too, that the Russian Black Sea fleet, normally held to around seven hundred ships, had been bolstered to twelve hundred, and the North fleet diminished to four hundred. One item stood out boldly. Inside a red-crayoned circle was the word *Vishakhapatnam*. Below it, "Primary Soviet Nuclear Offensive."

He noted that it was 10:25. "So long, Cockatoo, see you soon," and he went out to hunt up some more ice water. There were stirrings in the foyer now; uniforms flashed by, briefcases gleamed. The voices were only murmurs, though. Things were hushed, subdued.

Time, he thought. There was a re-check of his identification by the Marines, and he was waved into the parlor.

At first, he saw no one else. The room, with its meticulously arranged tropical motif, simply disappeared. All he saw, as he unconsciously tried not to falter in his stride, was Bernadette—her carefully smoothed hair, almost iridescent against the dark green of the wall behind her, her slim body, wrapped in white-linen delicacy, her casual, yet businesslike stance, as she held a sheaf of papers, chatting amiably with a nameless person to her left, her mid-heel white pumps terminating the graceful curve of her stocking-sheened calves. Bernadette.

Moser caught himself from calling out across the room to her, and snapped himself back to where he was, squelching the surprise, and turning instead to study the others around the room.

His mind whirred. *God damn,* he thought. What's going on here? Bernadette. The "Talbott Agreement." What's the connection?

He saw Chang to one side, and the Chinese stepped over to him. "Pretty elaborate here, isn't it?"

"I think I'll go nuts if I don't find out what the hell's going on soon," Moser said. "Looks like they really rolled out the carpet for you."

Chang nodded. "Let's sit over here."

Chang motioned to two rattan chairs in front of a long coffee table. Moser swung his briefcase onto its glossy, shellacked surface, and the chairs creaked as they sat down. Moser glanced at Bernadette.

She was the only woman in the room; Moser ticked off the names he knew, as if looking hurriedly through a telephone book. There was Stephenson; there was Dr. Harrison Haley from Seneca; there, in fact, was the Secretary of Defense Lawrence W. Golding; there was a five-star general whom Moser recognized as General Galanaugh, Chairman of the Joint Chiefs, and a colonel who was probably his aide. There was an admiral, and an Air Force general, and their aides. Chang sat stolidly beside Moser, relaxed but alert, a stereotype of an Oriental merchant in his white Palm Beach suit, his darkly angular face calm, frozen into a business smile reserved for magazine cover photographers.

Stephenson was talking in whispers with the Secretary of Defense. Galanaugh spoke casually with the admiral and the Air Force general. Moser heard the word "Saigon" repeated often. Bernadette spoke with one of the aides, while another shuffled through papers. Off in a corner, as inconspicuous as possible, sat a Navy commander, a black stenographic machine at his side.

The mood was almost too casual, Moser thought, as he unsnapped his briefcase; as if they were all members of an exclusive sailing club who had convened at a member's house for cocktails. Nevertheless, a peculiar excitement, a sense of urgency, permeated the room and belied the holiday atmosphere. Several of the attendees glanced at Chang repeatedly. Chang remained expressionless.

Stephenson stood up, one hand in his pocket; the other, resting on the back of a cushioned rattan chair, held his unlit pipe.

"If we'll come to order," he said officiously, "we can get the preliminaries over with. As most of you know, we've called this meeting because of a highly irregular turn of events. Our top Chinese agent, Mr. Chang Kwok-wah," Stephenson nodded in Chang's direction and heads turned again, "has found it necessary to leave Red China and has brought some urgent intelligence to our attention. What's more, as you'll learn in a few minutes, he has also brought out some unsettling strategic news. Information which, to put it bluntly, is extremely difficult to believe." Moser looked at Chang again, and admired his ability to remain impassive. Chang merely stared at the CIA Director.

"Let's go around the room once for Mr. Chang's benefit, please. General Charles F. Galanaugh, Chairman of the Joint Chiefs." Galanaugh nodded politely at Chang, and Chang returned an infinitesimal nod. "Admiral Simon Hughes, of the Joint Chiefs. General Adam Klein, of the Joint Chiefs." They were all smiling briefly at Chang as their names were called. Chang merely followed their faces around the room.

"Dr. Harrison N. Haley, of the Seneca Corporation in Los Angeles, who has been invited here because of the irregular nature of Mr. Chang's report, and who has been cleared to be briefed on this project by the Secretary of Defense." Haley smiled pleasantly, crossed his legs, but kept his gaze on Stephenson. "Miss Bernadette Talbott, whom you all know. Captain James Moser, formerly of Project RED MASK, and newly assigned as intelligence coordinator of the Seneca Corporation's Special Weapons Project. Captain Moser, gentlemen, de-briefed Mr. Chang yesterday."

Stephenson then turned to his side and nodded respectfully to the bespectacled gentleman beside him. "The Secretary of Defense, gentlemen." At this, they all bowed slightly, as the Secretary returned their silent acknowledgments.

"And Mr. Chang Kwok-wah." Stephenson extended his palm in Chang's direction.

"Now then," Stephenson continued as an aide began to pass out mimeographed sheets, "you're all receiving a detailed history of Mr. Chang's connection with our project. For Mr. Chang's edification, I'll briefly outline the terms of the Talbott Agreement, or what is known as Plan Nineteen.

"This Agreement is an alliance formed in 1959. Of course, there had been some interest and preliminary discussions before that. Mr. Eisenhower had discussed the possibility of such an alliance several times with Khrushchev at Camp David. Since 1959, no particular date of execution had been established until October 16, 1964. On that day, it will be recalled, Red China, in the Lop Nor area, exploded its first nuclear device. The day following, October 17, Nikita Khrushchev was deposed overnight as Premier of the Soviet Union and Aleksei Kosygin took control of the USSR and their military forces. It should be realized that this man is a hard and cold politician and has no intention of following the apparently peaceful and *quid pro quo* policies of the previous regime."

Chang felt himself leaning forward, his interest mounting as Stephenson continued.

"Then on May 14, 1965, China detonated their second device and afterward there were frantic communications between the President of the United States and Kosygin on the significance of that particular device to the balance of power at that time. That test proved the Chinese were well advanced over our intelligence reports and indeed much more sophisticated than we had presumed. Further, fallout patterns and dosages monitored by the Soviets and us revealed this was a device designed to generate ultrahigh amounts of radioactivity and probably the device was encased in Cobalt 90. Mr. Chang here has gone over our intelligence reports and indicated that these detonations were far more powerful than we had thought."

Chang tugged at his ear uncomfortably.

"It was at this time," Stephenson continued tutorially, "the decision was made to implement what is now referred to as the Talbott Agreement. This colloquial reference pertains to Miss Bernadette Talbott of Yale University, who, through her long-standing friendship with the then senator from Massachusetts, had proposed in a confidential treatise a possible solution for the containment of Red China vis-à-vis that nation's nuclear threat to the world. It was proposed that America enter into a binding military agreement with the Soviet Union, to undertake to guard the free world against Red China's potential, and, in fact, highly *probable,* nuclear aggression. The Talbott Agreement, Mr. Chang, is, in short, a plan to implement, some time around 1972, an armed and coordinated invasion of the Red China mainland and to seize control of that country's military and governmental actions. This, of of course, has been the most closely guarded secret this government has had, and naturally plans are already under way to effect the invasion on the date I've mentioned."

The enormity of Stephenson's words set Chang's mind reeling. My God, he thought, it's true! They are going to invade the Chinese mainland! He twisted in his seat and glanced at Moser. He was staring blankly ahead, biting his lip, and flicking his fingernails.

Moser looked up; the uniformed brass were eyeing him expectantly, waiting for his reaction. Then he turned and saw Bernadette. Her expression, too, remained unchanged. She lit another cigarette and listened as Stephenson continued.

"The initial step took place on June 9, 1965, precisely three weeks after China's second nuclear weapon was detonated at Lop Nor. This is when it was decided that American forces would be actively employed in the Far East, primarily Vietnam, because of its strategic position relative to the Chinese border.

"On June 17, 1967, China exploded her sixth test device, and nine days after that event, on June 26, Kosygin flew from Moscow and spent those eventful days with the former President in Glassboro. On August 3, Allied forces in the Far East were built to over a half million in accordance with the scheduling agreement for Plan Nineteen. This was because at the Glassboro meeting the formal agreement was signed and military coordinators alerted. General Galanaugh has been in constant contact with Marshal Yuri Kamovitch of the Soviet forces. Then on August 24, 1967, the agreement between the USSR and the United States to halt the spread of nuclear weapons was confirmed. In the following months, the Soviets announced that they had doubled their missile warheads, and finally, on September 29, the United States announced that it was expanding its offensive warheads to seventy-five hundred, including our new Perimeter Acquisition Radar and our Fractional Orbit Ballistic Re-entry Systems, known as FOBS. These announcements, paralleling each other, had to be made in order to couch our activities in some publicly palatable terms."

Moser was stunned into disbelief. He felt his muscles begin to relax, his confidence draining and his panic rising. The reality of the agreement was hitting hard. Had it finally come?

He looked at Chang and saw the narrowed eyes. Chang was no longer relaxed, instead nervously squeezing two fingers on his left hand. He looked impatient, anxious to have Stephenson finish and get his own comments into the conference. Bernadette's eyes quickly averted when Moser's met hers, as if she didn't want Moser to know she'd been watching his own reactions instead of Chang's. Moser turned back to Stephenson.

"It would probably be best to open this up to questions at this point," Stephenson went on, "and get right to the reasons you're with us today, Mr. Chang. Have you any comments?"

Chang didn't move for a long while, as the room fell silent and even the breathing of the conferees had been slowed to reduce any indication of anxiety. All eyes were on him. Moser saw the Oriental stir slowly.

Finally, Chang uncrossed his legs and lifted himself slowly from the chair. He stood erect and addressed himself to Stephenson, then glanced at each and every member of the meeting.

Chang was grim-faced. "I'm still trying to comprehend what you've just told me," he said. "Am I to believe now that the United States of America, jointly and with full military and financial support of the Soviet Union, will, for reasons you enumerate as world security and mutual survival, launch a full-scale air and ground invasion of the China mainland in 1972?"

Moser watched Stephenson's reaction. The older man

reached for another set of papers, unflinching at Chang's obvious disbelief.

"That's correct," Stephenson said coldly. "The move, designed by General Galanaugh and Marshal Kamovitch, will be a two-pronged, pincer-type movement of the sort used so effectively during World War II by British and American forces in the European theater.

"Russia will attack from the north, specifically from Sinkiang. Right now they have forces mounted on the Kyzyikun Desert. New, clean, but high-yield *Styx* missiles will be launched from the area of Vishakhapatnam, where their Black Sea fleet is mustered." Stephenson indicated the red-crayon circle with the stem of his pipe.

"The United States, after a feint toward North Korea, will launch its portion of the invasion from Vietnam, where our forces have been built up. It is planned to have a two-million man ground force in southeast Asia by 1972, and we will take the Hanoi route right through North Vietnam and into Kwangsi Province. At the same time, the force mustered on Taiwan—and this is still subject to negotiation with Generalissimo Chiang—will enter Fukien Province via Amoy. Further—and these, too, are only in the planning stage at this time, subject to agreement by the governments involved—American forces in South Korea, in combination with all the military resources of the Republic of Korea, will launch an air and naval armada directly through the Gulf of Chihli and into Tientsin. The object of that segment of the operation will be to seize the government coordination centers in Peking as soon as possible. When the security of Tientsin is effected, Phase One will be complete."

Chang sat down again, and slumped in his chair. Stephenson had taken his question as a lead into the exact details of the entire operational deployments. He decided to wait until this was over before voicing his next question.

"Phase Two," Stephenson went on, still jabbing at maps and charts with his pipe, "is designed as the convergence of all forces on Peking center target area. Clean nuclear devices will be employed exclusively, in order to permit immediate follow-up and occupation by ground and naval support forces. All NK-36 nuclear bombs have already been replaced with new lightweight and clean megatonage.

"Major support and supply functions will be through the Empire of Japan all during this implementation of the Agreement. Japan's constitutional commitment to refrain from participation in any armed conflict will be voided. She will cast her lot with us on realizing the ramifications and significance of what we must do, just as will West Germany, the United Kingdom, and other lesser powers.

"As of now, Phase Three is still being worked out. President Burgess has insisted on reconsidering any further action here. But what it will amount to is the splitting up of what is now mainland China. Chinese nuclear activities currently going at Lop Nor will be completely eliminated. Nationalist China, under General Chiang, will be granted one-fourth of the land area, in large part, eastern China. He will organize a viable, democratically-oriented government to restore to the Chinese people the dignity, the traditions, and the venerable social affairs which it has so pathetically lost since 1948. Russia now claims—and at this point we must place all credibility in their stated commitments—that she will be satisfied with a large portion of north and northwest China. The rest is still up to conjecture and in the hands of the President. You may assume for the moment, that post-conflict activities will closely resemble what was done with Berlin and Germany after World War II.

"This, briefly, is the general operational picture."

Chang, immediately rose. He jabbed a finger in the direction of the charts on the wall next to Stephenson. "If you'll pardon my bluntness," he said, "I think it will not be that easy. You speak as if we'll merely flick our collective finger and China will fall. What about counterattacks? What about China's military strength? It seems as if we may very well touch off a nuclear holocaust."

General Galanaugh then rose. Before he spoke, however, Stephenson, a bit disconcerted by the impending argument, held out both hands to take in the entire room

"Ah . . . we may as well open this up to general discussion. General?"

Galanaugh shifted the cigar in his mouth as he spoke. "It's not your station here, Mr. Chang, to question the plans and logistical strategy of the military. What you are here for, as I understand it, is to tell us exactly *what* such counterattacking strength will be. Namely, what *kind* of opposition we *will* run up against. Isn't that what you've been doing in China all along?"

Moser became more uncomfortable, and found himself nervously clicking his fingernails again. He saw Chang's shoulders square slightly, and knew the Chinese was holding back an intense frustration.

"General," Chang said evenly, "the mere fact that the Communists *know* about the plan should indicate that you'll meet much stronger opposition than you now plan to. If, that is, you are able to carry off the plan in the first place. My estimate is that Red China can force you to cancel the plan simply by calling diplomatic attention to it."

"Of course, anything can be denied, Mr. Chang," Galanaugh said, annoyed by Chang's condescending tone. "We all know the world never believes any claims Red China makes."

"Until they set off a nuclear device," Chang replied. "Or until they prove their claim to you."

Galanaugh withheld his comment for a few seconds, then sat down. "In any event," he said, "what we need from you is your estimate of what kind of resistance they'll throw at us."

Stephenson stepped in. "The resistance Mr. Chang is most concerned about is why we've invited Dr. Haley to this meeting. Mr. Chang wants us to believe Red China possesses a phenomenal psychokinetic ability which may force us to alter our plans."

"That's correct," Chang said. "There are a few select individuals who will be working under Dr. Tsien, as I told you yesterday, who can exercise remarkable PK powers, which could have vital strategic importance."

Galanaugh rose again, this time holding his cigar

tightly in his fingers as he spoke directly to Stephenson. "I saw that stuff out on the Coast," he said gruffly, "and I personally think more of some of the other Seneca developments than I do of that light beam project."

"The 'light beam project,' as you call it," Chang interrupted, "may be the most important thing out there. I'd personally like to review it, if I may."

Galanaugh was not to be put off. "I'll tell you one thing. It'll never replace the good old-fashioned bullet. I don't see how a man sitting in front of a laser could be compared to time-proven military weapons. Let's not forget, it's men and guns that win wars. It's bombs and planes that destroy enemies. Not people concentrating on moving things just by *thinking* about it." Galanaugh couldn't resist a slight chuckle, and both Moser and Chang registered their disapproval and disbelief with hard glares.

"What you don't seem to realize," Galanaugh went on, "is that we are fully committed to the Soviet Union. As much as they are to us."

Stephenson, seeing the growing friction, hastily interrupted the talk and gestured toward Dr. Haley. "Gentlemen, gentlemen," he began, "this is not the place to discuss the theory of war and tactics. Mr. Chang has brought us information that causes some concern here. It's our job to evaluate it and report to President Burgess. Which is why we asked Dr. Haley to fly here from the West Coast. I think it's more than evident that we must let Dr. Haley describe our own capabilities in this field, and for Captain Moser and Mr. Chang to evaluate the new information concerning the Chinese. Surely, if *we* are pursuing this field under government funds, there must be something to Mr. Chang's disturbing report."

"I'm afraid I don't share General Galanaugh's skepticism," Dr. Haley said. "Especially since he *has* seen it with his own eyes."

Galanaugh poked his cigar at Haley. "I'm not running *down* your projects, Dr. Haley. We are grown men acting in the best interest of our country. Of course, we must study all possibilities, but the President has assigned, and rightfully so I think, the military to prevent the free world from being strangled by the Chinese menace."

Chang's eyebrows raised indignantly. "You mean *nuclear* menace," he said softly.

Galanaugh nodded. "Of course. And when a missile is hurtling down on you, you are not going to sit down and just *think* about it."

"Not today," Chang said. "What I'm saying is, by 1972, if we all last that long, that may just be in the realm of possibility. Dr. Tsien is an amazing individual and he despises the United States. He has the ear of the highest Chinese militarists. He has all the money he needs, all the respect. I have personally witnessed some experiments that would seem incredible to you."

Secretary of Defense Golding broke in for the first time. "Gentlemen, it is obvious we're keeping Mr. Chang in the dark about our own capabilities in this peculiar field. Now, if indeed there is some military application, I think Mr. Chang could best evaluate it for us only after he has been thoroughly briefed on all of our special weaponry projects at Seneca. If you read the dossier before you, you know that Mr. Chang has been operating in the highest technical and government circles in China. It's for this reason that I'm charging Captain Moser to escort Mr. Chang to our West Coast facilities, and to have a complete detailed report and recommendation on my desk within forty-eight hours. Is that feasible, Captain?"

Moser swallowed. "Yes, sir. We can leave in the morning."

"Do you want anyone else to accompany you?"

Without looking, Moser could feel the presence of Bernadette. Bernadette Talbott. He pushed aside the urge to request that she accompany them, since she remained silent throughout the meeting, and he wasn't certain of her exact position. He decided against taking a chance and possibly embarrassing her. "No, sir," he said finally.

Stephenson looked at his watch. "Very well, then," he said. "Let's adjourn for lunch. We have a lot more ground to cover this afternoon."

The group stood up, almost in unison, as the military

men began talking animatedly and Stephenson turned to
huddle with the Secretary of Defense. Moser and Chang
collected their papers. Chang walked over to Dr. Haley
and bowed slightly as they shook hands and began talking. Moser, for the first time, caught Bernadette's eye,
and they strolled from the room together.

*   *   *

The dark, white-jacketed waiter brought Bernadette a
snifter of Courvoisier, and she watched him as he slowly
heated it over an exposed flame. Moser took another
drink of his Scotch, comfortable after the excellent dinner. They'd had fresh gulf shrimp in some sort of a white
wine sauce, fresh fruits and dates, and an accompanying
bottle of Krug's *Chenin Blanc*. Moser watched Bernadette, curious and admiring. The candle tossed golden
flickers of light onto her tanned skin. He liked what can-
dlelight did for a woman's features. Still gnawing at him,
however, was the extent of her involvement. Earlier, she
had calmly brushed aside his objections, playing down
her role, suggesting that it had become more consequen-
tial than she had intended. Moser fiddled with his drink,
swirling the ice idly with his finger.

"I want you to understand, Jim, that my part in this
thing is pretty minor. Aside from having proposed the original idea in a paper I once presented, I don't have any
active part in the plan, even though I do support it. They
keep me involved simply because I know about it. Other
than that, I'm just an international affairs consultant."

"You really support it? Now? Doesn't it seem to you a
pretty drastic alternative?"

"I believe it's our *only* alternative. Everybody knows
what's going to happen when China can deliver a bomb."

"It seems to me that everybody *thinks* they know
what's going to happen. After all, remember the Rosen-
bergs? We were all going to be wiped out by Russia that
time. Now you've got us buddy-buddy in a nuclear plot."

Bernadette shrugged her shoulders. "Did you bring me
here to argue, or may I have another brandy?"

Moser motioned for the waiter. "I'm sorry. Things

happen pretty fast around here, and after twelve years of living with Orientals, one changes his perspective. I'm really concerned that the military power of this country has gotten out of hand."

"Jim," she said, "please. That was a long time ago, when this idea, for me, was only a theory on paper. Now, I just don't know. My head is swimming. From the brandy. From this day. From everything."

"Do you want to go?"

"No. I want to know more about you. What are you like?"

"Friendly, courteous, kind—and seldom obedient. I hate routine, love girls." He grinned at her.

Bernadette looked up and reached for a cigarette. "Is there a girl, Jim?" She was momentarily embarrassed and groped for the right words. "I mean, is there someone you . . ."

"Nah. You've already forgotten. My life before this was in Little Shanghai. I had girlfriends there. One of whom I loved very much. She's gone. You become extremely fatalistic about it. Instant love becomes a necessity. No attachments are possible. Is the same question appropriate for you?"

She smiled at him. "No one. No one permanent. No one I want to become permanent. The men I meet are shallow and flaccid, or ambitious and racing for the top and anxious and ruthless in their determination to get there. Nobody wants to go to museums anymore. Nobody wants to slow down."

The waiter brought the brandy and they both fell silent, watching him rotate it above the flame. "Do you like to swim?" Moser asked her.

"I love it. You are looking at the star of the Bryn Mawr Swim Club."

"Since you're an old hand at secret meetings in lush tropical settings, I thought you might be able to show me the delights of tropical moonlit waters."

"Am I being propositioned?"

"Only for a swim. The rest is up to you."

Moser watched the candle throw amber lights into the turquoise eyes. "I didn't bring my bikini," she said.

Moser grinned at her. "Neither did I."

*   *   *

The open convertible wove smoothly down to the cove, drenched in moonlight. The air was still, the beach deserted, and the water was a million shining dimes. There was a sound of waves nibbling softly at the shore-line as they got out of the car. Now, barefoot, they sank into the sand, still warm from the sun. Bernadette suddenly ran ahead, toward the water, splashing in, ankle-deep. He chased her, catching her finally, breathless, and kissed her fully, tasting her mouth.

She broke away. "Come on, I want to show you this place. I feel as if it all belongs to me. . . ." She took his hand and led him into a small cove. "See? Look at the sea from here." She sat on the weathered trunk of a tree, and motioned him to her. "I love it here," she said. "It really is like paradise. Everyone moves slowly here. The few people are real. Unpretentious. Just people, not politicians."

Moser toyed with a slender piece of driftwood, tracing roads in the deep sand, watching moonlight throw distorted shadows over the cove. Then he tossed the stick aside. "I thought we were going to swim, not philosophize."

"Sorry. I just get that way here. Besides, I really don't have a bikini hidden away. And I think I'm bashful."

"That doesn't fit very well with your philosophy. I thought you were the unassuming type. Honest in word and deed."

"I know, but . . ."

"But what? We promised ourselves a swim. We don't need bathing suits."

"What about you?"

He stood up, pulling off his tie and flicking open the buttons of his shirt. "Let's go. This moonlight will do even more for you than those candles at dinner!"

Bernadette rose to him and turned her back. "Help

me," she said. He slid the zipper fastener down, and she stepped out of the dress. Neatly, she lay it on the tree trunk. Her smooth legs gleamed in the moonlight as she unsheathed them from her stockings. Then she paused. "You're ogling me."

"I'd be crazy if I didn't." He reached out and pulled her close to him, not quite touching. Then he unfastened her bra and let it fall. Her breasts were ivory beneath the tanned shoulders, the nipples already erect without his touch.

Moser pulled her against him and felt her breath warm in his ear. He slid his palms behind her, onto her buttocks, firm under the wisp of lingerie. He kissed her gently, then with a sudden urgency, and he slipped his hands beneath the silk.

She drew the top of her body away from him, but kept pressed hard against him from her waist down, with an urgency all her own. "Oh, Jim," she whispered. "It's all sand, and it's so . . ."

". . . sandy," he finished for her. "Come on." He shed his clothes hurriedly and grasped her hand, pulling her toward the water. "Come on," he said again.

"Why? Do you know what you're doing?"

"Sure," he grinned at her. "Experimenting." They splashed into the gently rolling surf, hand in hand.

"What is this, the equivalent of a cold shower?" she said.

Buoyed by the cool water, they hovered like two gleaming fish. He held her close, searching her softnesses. "Nope, it's play, and it's fun, and it's. . . ." But his voice went throaty as he thrust into her. Tightly, he held her against him, flipped over, and capsized in the moon-sparkled sea. They went down, giggling, the tension eased. Then, "Come on," he said. "I'll race you to the float before we drown!"

He beat her by seconds, noted with relief that there were chaise pads on the structure, and reached down a helping hand for her to climb aboard.

The intensity of their embrace was explosive. Water droplets on their skin skidded into each other, and the wet bodies glistened in the moonlight. The bay lapped longingly at the float as they lost themselves in each other's arms.

CHAPTER SIX

On the flight from Miami, Chang fell asleep almost as soon as the plane reached altitude. He had been up most of the night listening to Dr. Haley's excited descriptions of the progress being made at Seneca, and both his mind and body welcomed the soporific, gentle whine of the jet engines. The doctor himself was asleep beside him, his head nodding languidly with the occasional rise and fall of the craft as it burrowed through the turbulence outside. They were all tired. Only Moser couldn't sleep. He peered out through the tropical squall, through the droplet-beaded window off the starboard wing. All around he could see flashes of blue-white forked lightning among the dark-grey and violet clusters of storm clouds, reminding him of a battlefield in Asia, with firecracker lights and thunderous mortar claps dotting the atmosphere. It was a parody of a Chinese New Year celebrated in a low, thick fog.

The jet shuddered and shook, buffeted by the invisible hands of wind that pushed and pulled it through the squall. And then, suddenly, they were out of it, sweeping across a vast, blue stretch of the Gulf of Mexico, calm and placid under the clear morning sky that reached down to shut out the storm behind them. He looked over at Chang and Dr. Haley. Their heads rolled silently as the plane banked to adjust its course, as if they were buoyed up in their sleep by a preservative fluid, cuddled and calmed in an aqueous suspension that rested their bodies and lay dormant their thoughts.

"I wish I could sleep like that," Moser half-whispered

to himself. I wish, I wish, he continued in thought, and his mind wandered forward to the cockpit where the crew expertly guided the big jet—and he'd had his chance, once, in cadet training; a choice of flight school or the assignment in Formosa. But there was something in him then, some youthful, arrogant assurance that he could learn the ways of the Orient and do something to help this stricken mass that was dying on humanity's doorstep. But now? Maybe the world would be better off if he were only a pilot.

Or a musician. Someday he wanted to study music. Once he had planned to enter the San Francisco Conservatory and study under a master guitarist, perhaps even travel to Spain and learn the classic Flamenco techniques of Sabicas or Serrano. He had wanted to teach, too. And that, at least, he had done. When he could forget the macabre purpose of his pedantry, he had enjoyed the combination of teaching and expressing his love of the Orient that Little Shanghai had given him. And, joke as he would about his "twelve years in confinement," Moser would cherish those years and yearn for them often.

But of all the things he had wanted to do, being a party to the Talbott Agreement wasn't one of them. Whatever his role in living, his visions were of a different sort of life, a life where villagers in China and fishermen in Portugal and concrete-shrouded businessmen in New York would all understand and accept each other, would have the time and the freedom to do as they pleased or as they were inspired or as they were driven. But instead he saw the villagers running amid flames, the fishermen drowning in the waves that fed them, the businessmen falling fathoms down through steel canyons until they thudded to futile death on the senseless and insensible ground of politics.

He thought of Bernadette. How typically inane that she had been caught up in this, in a maelstrom of military stupidity that had seized her floating straw and built it into a ship of doom. Do we have to restrict our thoughts? Moser mused. Must we be afraid to test a sophomoric theory, voice a tentative opinion, for fear some warped

and twisted brain might distort and bend it into a tool of
war? The theme of her book, after all, was merely national behavior. Perhaps the horror of it was its accuracy.
She had theorized that nations irrevocably became a collective, childish brain, predictably behaving as children
do, heedless of the adult wisdom of a minority of its cells,
guided less by reason than by a cruel, corporate instinct.
And the action her nation had taken had proved her
theory—grasping at her hypothetical recipe for world survival as if it were testament, instead of an exercise in political psychology.

What could he and Chang do about it? Why had
Chang been so reticent in discussing his psychokinetic
ability when all he had to do was let the authorities know
what the Chinese could do, and maybe scare hell out of
them? Perhaps Seneca would bring the answer. He found
himself growing impatient to see what Chang would think
of the myriad projects and developments budding in the
hills of Santa Monica. Because the words Moser would be
putting to paper hours from now might very well spell out
the future of China, the future of a society bent on destroying itself in the name of security: "Yes, Mr. Secretary, we can confidently go in and bomb hell out of China
without killing more than a few million people." Or, "No,
Mr. Secretary, we cannot go in and wipe out Red China
because if we do we'll get wiped out ourselves." Or, "I
don't know, Mr. Secretary, I guess we'll just have to wait
and see whether the missiles come flying across the
ocean at us, hurtling through the crystalline ionosphere
as their sleek bodies search out cities, their voracious ap-
petites for death growing stronger with each mile."

Jesus Christ, Moser said to himself as he, too, started
dropping off to sleep. Why the hell can't they get someone else for this thing? Send me back to the Sangre de
Cristo Mountains, where no one wants to drop bombs.

*   *   *

A dark, polished Department of Defense Buick sedan
slipped through the early morning traffic as the bright
Santa Monica sun burned down through the fog. Inside,
an armed Marine lieutenant guided the car mechanically

and a sergeant sat silently beside him, puffing a stubby cigarette. Finally, the car stopped in front of a small, pink tract home and honked once.

Like an automatically actuated robot, Mike Fowler stepped to the front door and opened it quickly, kissed his housecoated wife, skipped down the steps toward the waiting car. He was a wiry, curly-haired young man in a J. C. Penny cotton shirt and blue slacks. His loafers were scuffed, and the heels of his white crew socks were wearing thin. He walked on the balls of his feet, lightly, giving his gait a springy bounce rather than a determined stride. He grinned at the two Marines and commented casually about the weather, but received only a stolid glance from the lieutenant and a curt nod from the sergeant.

The car rolled off smoothly, passed the service station at Santa Monica Boulevard and Ocean Drive, where Michael Fowler worked during the evenings. Then it picked up speed, wove through busy intersections and climbed the oceanside hills toward the massive, western-styled buildings that housed the prestigious Seneca Corporation. It was a few minutes before nine as the car stopped, the Marines opened the rear door, and Fowler hopped out eagerly. They escorted him to the security office where he was issued his special badge and surrendered the contents of his pockets.

He had gone through the same procedure every morning for the past eleven months, but each time seemed new, held a special thrill in the courtesies extended to him, in the importance he felt in the midst of the white-smocked scientists and their complex instruments. For although Mike Fowler was an ordinary young man, a junior college dropout who had legitimized his unborn son with a fast trip to Las Vegas, he was a small but highly essential part of the complex Seneca project known as DEIMOS.

The two Marines escorted Fowler down a network of hallways to the door of a small laboratory. Here he was signed in again and his coded plastic card inserted methodically into a crackle-grey box. A red lamp flashed above the steel door and Fowler walked into the laboratory office alone. It was empty. "I guess Dr. Haley ain't back yet," he said to himself, and strolled around the office. It was small and spartan with a steel desk of the type often seen in cost-plus-fixed fee companies which have to watch their expenses. Beside it was a plastic-covered couch and a low table piled with old magazines. And nothing else—except in the far corner, where stood an old, paint-chipped pinball machine—"Balley's Double-Eight."

Mike walked over to it and dropped in a dime. He slid back the handle and spun a ball into the center of the gaudy bumpers. It flopped noisily for a few seconds, then rolled down along a row of holes. Mike tensed. The ball bounced toward the "Free Game" lane and then away. And then it hovered and, as Mike gave the machine a tap with the heel of his hand, the ball seemed to climb deliberately back toward the lane.

"Playing games again, are you, my boy?"

Mike turned, startled, and the ball sagged and rolled down, finding its inevitable path to the "Out" hole. He looked at the sharp-jawed young engineer who stood there eyeing him officiously. "Ain't Doc Haley back yet?" he asked.

"Pretty quick," Bob Stuart replied, "and you've got a big day ahead of you, a big day."

Mike winced at the condescending tone of the young man's voice. He got along fine with Dr. Haley. Haley was older and kind of like a father. But this guy was probably not much older than Mike, and whenever he was around he made Mike feel like some sort of an animal. Besides, he always talked to Dr. Haley in big long engineering words and numbers Mike could never understand.

"I'm ready for anything," said Mike, squaring his shoulders. "I feel real good this morning."

"You'd better be," the engineer answered with only a half smile. "We've got some pretty important people coming to watch your show." Then he turned and led Mike into a small, specially built copper-insulated research chamber, the heart of the project called DEIMOS.

Engineer Bob Stuart laced his stubby fingers together

and cracked the heels of his hands with a hollow, popping sound. "Well, let's give our little magic mind some practice, shall we?" he asked in a brusque tone that turned the question into an order, and sat down behind a broad console on which lights twinkled and gleamed in parti-colored array. He flicked a switch.

Mike Fowler sat down in the cage designed to shield him from any spurious electromagnetic fields. The lights dimmed, and a readout screen above the cage flashed "LASER POWER ON." A needle-beam of coherent ruby light cut across the cage to a rectangular ground-glass screen. A reticle on the screen formed a red circle with smaller green circles arranged concentrically within it. Each colored band marked a thin circle of selenium, each connected to a cabinet behind the screen. The laser beam hit in a tiny splash of red light at the center of the small-est green circle, exactly six centimeters in diameter.

"Okay," Stuart said crisply, "the timer will begin in five seconds. Watch the readout. This trial will be two minutes and you will attempt a three centimeter devia-tion."

Mike Fowler looked up at the flickering readout tubes. "READY." Then the neon symbols flicked to "IN PROG-RESS" and Mike turned to a hard, sweating concentra-tion on the sparkling red dot on the screen.

*　　*　　*

The Boeing 707 swooped down on Los Angeles Inter-national Airport, cushioning itself to a soft landing through the thick, hot smog. Impatiently, Dr. Haley and Chang were among the first to debark, with Moser bring-ing up the rear. A few minutes later they were in a rented Chevrolet on a grey ribbon of freeway. Dirty, brown Los Angeles sprawled around them. As they turned onto the San Diego Freeway and started toward the Santa Monica Mountains, a salty Pacific breeze began to disperse the eye-watering smog.

They reached the Seneca Corporation about thirty min-utes later and Chang, for the first time, saw the research facility that was to sire a whole new generation of weap-

onry. The low, beige buildings spread before him in re-
petitive angles, windowless walls of Palos Verdes stone
and tilting roofs of crushed white rock. From the outside
it gave no hint of what its walls concealed. It could have
been an oilman's estate—or a Hollywood star's winter
hideaway. Only the anodized aluminum block letters over
the glass-paneled entrance identified its real occupant.
They said simply: "SENECA."

Through the balance of the morning they were led
through the many-faceted laboratories and *inner sancta* of
hidden workshops. Moser went along impatiently. He had
seen most of the facility a week before when he had arrived to accept his new assignment as DEIMOS coordinator, and resented the time wasted in nonessential sightseeing. But he knew better than to try to derail the
smooth-rolling train of the "Official tour procedure." And
before long he was taking a new interest in many of the
details he had missed on his first trip.

In one division, they saw a mockup of a huge nuclear-
powered underwater troop carrier. In another, they
showed Chang what Seneca was doing in holography, the
new area of research that uses coherent light to recon-
struct three-dimensional pictures. This, he was told, was
part of a long-range addition to Peripheral Acquisition
Radar. Another lab revealed a small personal combat
computer designed to be used by infantrymen and linked
directly to a master brain at battalion headquarters. This,
in turn, was fed directly to a central control and gave
field commanders a constant, accurate fix on every man.
In yet another area, Chang was given a demonstration of
a personal defoliator—a hand grenade-sized capsule filled
with a powerful herbicide.

Then Moser and Chang were led into a large, round-
walled room that contained an enormous tank of water in
which four wet-suited men were busy constructing their
own living quarters. They were told that the men had
been in the tank for seven days, living entirely off the
plants and the various seafoods in the ecologically-bal-
anced tank. They were testing the new human gill and

were receiving their oxygen directly from the water. One of them waved at Moser.

At one point, they entered an elevator and descended to a long, metallic tube, through the slotted glass windows of which they saw various animals, large and small, simply lying on the ground. The animals, they were told, were in a state of suspended animation brought on by a new Freon-related gas which could be shot from an ordinary pistol. The animals would remain in this zombie state for twenty-four hours after they were shot.

One of the most bizarre developments they saw was a human in a small round tank of water. He was chatting with a dolphin. Over the intercom, they heard the man saying, "Are you ready for lunch now, Coco?"

They then heard a series of high-pitched beeps from a loudspeaker, immediately followed by a shrill but recognizable series of unmodulated words. They sounded much like the electronic voice transducers used by laryngectomy victims. "Not yet," the speaker buzzed. "Let's play ball first."

Chang was fascinated. "Is that the dolphin?"

Haley grinned at him. "Certainly is. Remarkable, isn't it?"

Moser watched the dolphin leap after the rubber ball and return it to the man in the tank.

"You see," Haley explained, "this is something the Navy boys at China Lake and Dr. Lily in Florida have helped us with. Seneca has been able to discriminate between the dolphin's sounds and modulate them into a discernible language. Pete, in there, is talking directly to Coco. They can actually sit and chat with each other for hours on end, although the vocabulary is still rather limited."

Chang couldn't help but laugh. "What the devil do you talk to a dolphin about, anyway?"

"You'd be surprised," Haley said. "That one has a hang-up on a male we've got in another tank, and keeps nagging the trainer to let her visit. We have another dolphin who likes Western films. We've been showing him *High*

Noon and *Shane* until we're sick of them, but he cheers and moans in the same scenes every time. He loves it!"

"But let's move on," Haley said, starting for the door. "Let's have lunch and then get to DEIMOS."

*   *   *

Mike Fowler sat in his copper mesh cage and stared at the target before him, resting between periods of intense concentration. In the isolation of his sound-proof cell he couldn't notice the approach of three visitors who quietly took their seats behind the one-way glass panel to the right of the control console.

As Chang and Moser settled in their seats, Dr. Haley turned and looked at his guests. "When the engineer gives the signal, gentlemen, Mr. Fowler will begin to concentrate his thoughts on that beam of red laser light. If he succeeds in moving the spot into one of the target areas, a bell will sound. Perhaps, by way of explanation, I should say that the human body emanates or transmits, if you will, certain waves or energy particles which seem to behave like electromagnetic energy. Exactly what they are, we still don't know, but what we are trying to do here is to channel these energies—the 'Psi Factor,' as we call it, into something tangible. Crude as it is, our experiment will prove that these energies do exist and, perhaps more important, that they can be improved upon by exercise.

"On that point, let me say something else. You're probably familiar with some of the early work with paranormal mental powers—Zener Card guessing, and that sort of thing? Well, with that system a subject didn't know if he had done well until a statistician had gotten around to analyzing the scores. Compare that, if you will, to an athlete trying to master the high jump without a visible cross bar! That's why the most important scientific development we have here is a simple bell. When it rings, Mike—our young subject there—*knows* what he has accomplished, and that knowledge helps him strengthen his effort. Without such a tangible 'reward,' progress would be impossible. It's like I used to tell some of my esteemed colleagues at Duke—'My God, man, how can you expect someone to learn to wiggle his ears if you don't give him a mirror!' "

As Dr. Haley was chuckling over his nice parallel, Bob Stuart's voice crackled over the intercom, announcing the resumption of another test. A light flashed on the numerical readout: "READY." Then the numbers flickered to: "IN PROGRESS." Mike stared again at the sparkling red dot. Seconds passed slowly as interest mounted, eyes fixed on the target screen. Beads of sweat on Mike's forehead trembled and fell, and even the implacable Haley, in the relative comfort of the observation room, reached for his own handkerchief.

The spot continued to stare back at Mike and the watchers, unmoving. Stuart coughed nervously behind the console, and because he had left the switch of the intercom in the "On" position, the cough clapped like a mortar shell in the room beyond. Then the time buzzer sounded.

Haley pushed his "Talk" switch. "What is it, Stuart? Something wrong in the grounding, there?"

"It checks out, sir," the engineer replied, startled to hear his superior's voice.

"What about it, Mike?" Haley asked, cutting him off, "do you feel all right?"

"Dr. Haley?" Mike said loudly into his own microphone. "Glad you're back. Yeah, I've been having a little trouble. Let me try again, okay?"

"Sure, Mike," Haley answered in a fatherly tone. "Take it easy for a minute, then give it another go. You'll do fine." .

Haley closed the talk switch and turned to his guests. "A lot of things can affect this 'Psi Factor,' as you can readily see. Maybe Mike's a little upset, because after all, he's a human being, not a machine."

Then the room was silent again and Mike Fowler's perspiration returned as the engineer signaled another test. The spot still stood defiantly in the center of the target screen. But then, after forty seconds, it flickered and moved slowly off the center dot. It crept imperceptibly toward the first small green circle.

Haley watched excitedly as Moser leaned forward. As the spot approached the first green circle, three centimeters off center, Fowler was drenched. The collar of his cotton shirt was limp and dark with moisture. Dr. Haley watched with almost equal concentration, clenching his teeth in a way that sent ripples along his glistening jowls.

The sharp, startling sound of the bell broke through the room, shattering the eggshell of tension. Dr. Haley stood up suddenly, unashamedly relieved.

"Fine, Mike," he said, reaching for the switch. "Now relax for a minute." He turned back to his guests. "You have just seen a three centimeter deviation. What do you think?"

He watched Chang closely, awaiting his reaction. Moser, too, looked expectantly at Chang.

Chang narrowed his eyes, puzzled. "What do I *think*? About what?"

Haley shrugged and waved one palm at the Faraday Cage. "About our project, of course. How does it seem to you?"

Chang stood up. His quizzical expression gradually turned to surprise, almost to shock. "You mean that's *it*? *That's* the project?"

Haley sputtered, searching for words. "Well, we've done some other things. Mike has a pinball machine that he can . . ."

"Not a *pin*ball machine," Chang interrupted sarcastically. "Is that all you really do? Move a laser beam off target and fool with pinball machines?"

"Of course, we're just getting started," Haley fumbled. He began to sense the hint of what Chang was about to say and seemed afraid to hear the truth. "There's a great deal more than can be done . . . and Mike can already do much better than this. . . ."

Chang brushed past him to the door leading to the Faraday Cage. "Have him turn on the laser," he called back over his shoulder. Haley barked a command over the intercom, and in seconds the Nixie tubes glared their message. Chang concentrated as the ruby beam hovered on the target. Then the red dot on the screen moved quickly through three rings, clanging the bell in rapid succession, and then it wavered around the full circle, darting in and out of the target rims. The bell clanged incessantly until Moser thought the persistent noise would drive him crazy. Dr. Haley's mouth was open.

"Okay, okay," Moser called through the still open door, and Chang's shoulders dropped in relaxation. The beam snapped back to dead center, as if someone had suddenly cut a big rubber band.

"My God," Moser said to him. "It looks like what we're doing here is peanuts. Why didn't you explain this to Stephenson at Walker's Cay?"

"Because of that goddamned general what's-his-name," Chang said. "I had to know where you people were on this thing before I made a fool of myself and jeopardized the credibility of my story." Chang rose and slapped his sides. "Good God, doesn't anybody realize what you've got hold of here?" He avoided embarrassing Haley with a direct look, and gazed sternly at Moser. "What do you think moves those photons, mumbo-jumbo? No! Something *stronger* than a photon—even when it comes directly and unaccelerated from the head of an untrained boy who couldn't even make the scrub team in Peking. I can do fifty times what he can—and Dr. Tsien has a capacity of 8.3, *mao-pao-li-lian*, about ten times stronger by actual measurement.

"But that's nothing. That's without acceleration." Chang shook his head in exasperation, and finally looked directly at Dr. Haley. "Not too long ago Dr. Tsien and I completely annihilated a low-flying fighter plane and a bomber flying at 7,000 feet, and we used the most elementary prototype equipment.

"What you've got here is a bullet, gentlemen, perhaps the most potentially powerful bullet imaginable. But you're playing around trying to shoot it out of a popgun!"

"Good Lord!" Haley said, still shaking his head. "You shot down aircraft? But how do you do it?"

"Have you got a blackboard?" Chang asked.

"Certainly. In my office," Haley replied, moving to the door. "Stuart, can you come in here?" The four moved into Haley's office. After introducing his engineering assistant, Haley unfolded two tin chairs for his guests, and Chang stepped to the blackboard and wiped the eraser across the already cleaned board as he tried to collect his thoughts.

"All right," he began, as he picked up the chalk and drew a Chinese symbol on the slate surface, "you talk about 'Psi Factor.' We call it *mao-pao-li-lian*. In the current ideological patois that translates as 'brain-wave-strength units.' But the name isn't important. What *is* important is that we deal with it in *units;* we apply quantum physics to something you're still treating like some kind of magic. Now, I'm not saying that we know what it is. I don't know what an electron is, do you? But we know how it may behave—and we're beginning to find out how to control it.

"Look," he said, facing them directly, "I read about a device you developed a year or so ago. It's an 'electron saw' that employs a simple cathode emitter and a magnetic field accelerator. Now, an electron is practically nothing, right? And yet your published reports said it could cut through four inches of solid stone. All right, then, look at this." Chang turned back to the blackboard and soon had it filled with a schematic diagram. The symbols were standard, and yet somehow—perhaps because he seemed to hold the chalk as if it were a Chinese calligrapher's brush, the finished drawing had a strangely Oriental beauty.

"This is the lens," he said, pointing to one section, "which focuses the Psi-units into a coherent force. Then the field—here—arranges the random emanations into a flow which doesn't disturb their original wave direction. Then, here's the accelerator. A miniature cyclotron, no more, no less, right? But that's all we need. The Psi-units are trapped in here for five to ten nanoseconds, until they achieve escape velocity. Then they're discharged here, through a final lens.

"Now, presumably we could do the same sort of thing with electrons or photons or any type of particle that is affected by a field. But Psi-units have something more going for them. First, they're more powerful—and we've got the dust that used to be two airplanes lying in the desert to prove that. Second, they're not electronic slaves, they're emanations of the mind—and they go where they're directed, even after acceleration! Any questions?" Chang turned to survey three wrinkled brows, three open mouths.

Moser spoke first. "Chang," he said soberly, "doesn't this mean that you could put up a ring of these things, like a wall around China, and, given enough trained operators, simply *think* anything out of the sky we may throw at them?"

"That's exactly the point, Jim," Chang answered, visibly relieved that someone seemed to understand. "That's why I'm here. That's why I got out when I heard about this 'Agreement.' It's a godsend that I was the one Dr. Tsien chose to help him in this. Because with this capability the Red Chinese can immobilize any offensive equipment you now have, or that you're even contemplating. Everything I've seen here can be made obsolete by a single well-trained PK specialist."

"Well," Haley hesitated, "what do you say, Bob?"

The young engineer rubbed his hands nervously along the sharp edge of his jaw. "The circuitry certainly appears to be feasible, sir," he answered tentatively, "but I feel I have to take issue on one point. Now, I'm willing to postulate that thought waves exist and that they will respond to a field. That's why we had to construct the Faraday Cage, after all. But we have found that any field at all simply destroys Mike's ability to function because thought waves are so much weaker than electrical emissions. Now, I don't doubt Mr. Chang's sincerity, but I find it impossible to believe that anyone can display the kind of mental power that could actually take advantage of an electrical field. Perhaps the influence of Oriental philosophy. . . ." He flushed as he groped for words, and looked at Chang, leaning placidly against the blackboard. There was a half-smile on his face but a fixed stare in his eyes, and just the faintest wrinkle of concentration on his smooth, Chinese forehead. "Well, no offense," Stuart continued, "but the kind of power you're talking about is too much to accept, in spite of the demonstration you put on a few minutes ago. I'm a scientist and, pardon me, but the modern Western mind is trained to reject the—"

His throat closed on the next word, and only a Germanic glottal stop escaped as a relay suddenly clicked in the corner of the room. Haley glanced up from his desk, expecting to find that Mike Fowler had come in to while away his time at the pinball machine. But no one was there. Only Chang, now standing erect some five feet away in front of the blackboard, his shoulders hunching as he stared directly at the machine. Another relay clicked, then another and another. The "Free Game" light flashed on. Then, in sequence, the "B-A-L-L-E-Y" of the title lights blinked across the gaudy glass screen. The game counter started to move, faster and faster, until it was clocking free games at a high-pitched whine. Finally, a bell rang and a big red panel lit up with the word "TILT." Chang folded his arms and turned to the trio. "Well," he said, repeating himself, "any questions?"

*   *   *

Moser made a hasty call to Stephenson reporting what he had just seen Chang do; then he and Chang left immediately for March Air Force Base to take a special jet back to Washington.

Along the Santa Ana Freeway traffic was beginning to grow heavier as various early shifts were being let off from the many plants and manufacturing buildings. Finally, Chang broke his silence and turned to Moser.

"Sorry I took you by surprise, Jim," he said, "but I couldn't let anyone know until I was sure of our own capabilities. I have to make them believe me."

"I know you do, and that's what's bothering me," Moser replied, not turning his head from the road. "I can hardly believe it myself."

"Well, look," Chang said, "it's not that big a deal, actually. All I did was regulate an electron flow. The machinery takes care of itself. You can't over-dramatize this thing, Jim. You can't look only at the effect and forget about the actual cause."

"They can't go through with it," Moser said suddenly.

"I know," Chang said, staring out the window. "I have to convince them it won't work."

"We can," Moser said, holding the wheel firmly as they passed the slower traffic. "We can do it together."

"How? It's obvious General Galanaugh and the Joint Chiefs have their whole effort behind it. We seem to be committed all the way up to the Secretary of Defense, and even with the Russian bigwigs."

"That's just what's bothering me," Moser said. "But Galanaugh's just a prick general. He can be ignored, I think. And we don't have to stop at the Secretary of Defense, either."

Chang turned to Moser, who was manipulating the car into a parking slot at the Base. His eyes widened in a question, then he nodded as he realized the meaning of Moser's words. "Yes," he said. "Get to the *one* person who should be able to see the consequences of putting this 'Agreement' into motion now. Right?"

Moser snapped off the ignition and yanked up the brake. "That's it," he said. "Take it right to the President."

* * *

They had little delay at March Air Force Base, and before long Air Force 126 was streaking along at 650 miles per hour. They were alone on the plane, and sipped coffee out of styrofoam cups as an airman second class brought them each a box lunch. The craft rocketed along, leaving white contrails over the Arizona desert.

They talked about days at Little Shanghai, trying to relax, to let the tension-fibers of their bodies loosen as they settled down for the four-and-a-half hour trip to Washington.

Moser kidded, tossing questions about the Chinese women, and a smirking Chang filled him in on all the details. Chang, on the other hand, insisted on nearly a play-by-play indication of the L.A. Dodgers' last seven seasons. Then he grew nostalgic as he spoke of San Diego and the long-gone family ties.

"It's hard to believe you're really Mexican," Moser said.

"Outside of saying *uno más cerveza, por favor,* or *uno más martini sobre rocas con poquito vermouth,* I couldn't even find my way around Tijuana anymore. But I've got no regrets, Jim. I've done something that only two or three people out of billions on the earth have been able to do."

Moser swirled the dregs of his cup. "You sure as hell have. Aren't you looking forward to getting out of this and living a normal life?"

"Any life I lead from now on would *not* be a normal life, I assure you. I'll have to take on another identity—which reminds me. Something I've often wondered about. Whatever happened to my namesake—Chang Kwokwah?"

"Funny you should mention that. I thought of him when I read your dossier the other night. Nothing, I guess. He's still working under the name of Stanley Wong, as a draftsman for a lock-making firm in Vancouver. Happy as a clam, I bet."

Moser picked up an apple and looked at his friend. "When this is all over, Chang, do you want to stay in America?"

Chang looked up and frowned. "I guess so," he said, hesitantly.

"Look, pal. What I'm asking you, do you have a girl over there?"

"I have. Or did. And I know what you're thinking. She's the daughter of the Minister of Transportation. Number three daughter. And right now, her father is having my ancestry confirmed, since we've been talking about marriage."

"That's sticky."

"Yeah, but that was six months ago. It takes months and months for the families to consult all the old books, big dusty things with heavy red covers. The signs of the zodiac are consulted. Fortunately, the Chang family has an immaculate astrological and genealogical back-ground."

"You miss her, I take it."

"Sure, I miss her. I would have married her until this damn thing came out."

Moser put down his apple and opened a small container of milk. "This damn thing," he repeated. "What the hell are we going to do?"

"Not much we can do, Jim. Certainly, Chinese experts would be overruled by the big guns. Your friend Bernadette and your previous administration didn't quite accurately estimate the tenacity of the Chinese."

"No matter how we present the report, I don't think it's going to change their minds."

"It doesn't seem like it. But we've got to do something to, at least, stall them."

"Well, for God's sake, it seems to me that once they realize what you and Tsien can do, they'd know how far behind we are in PK capability. Whether or not this would be enough to make them alter their position, or at least modify it to something less drastic, I don't know."

Chang sipped from his cup, considering his words. "Who knows? It could be the Soviets. Have you thought of that? They have more to gain from the containment of China than the United States. Hell, they're next-door neighbors, and we're half a world away. I know for a fact that the Russians are really afraid the Chinese will march right through Mongolia."

"Will they?"

"I don't know, Jim. But it'll be a long time before the Red Chinese have long-range tactical capability. Right now, their big concern is making the 'Great Leap Forward' mean little more than a stroll across the street."

"Yeah, but what's that got to do with pouring all the money into Tsien's work?"

"Defense. China has no capability now for defense against an invasion or an attack. Nothing. Outside of Tsien and myself, they have no real capability. But after the demonstration a week ago, he's certain to get everything he needs. And once Tsien gets a core of specialists trained and on the job, they could do it almost overnight. Besides that, Jim, remember they know about the Talbott Agreement, and that could be diplomatically fatal."

"They couldn't prove such an agreement existed. Hell, their credibility gap is wider than ours. All the United States and Russia would have to do is ignore it. Make them out as a paper tiger. They have absolutely no proof."

Chang looked up. "All they'd need is a single document. A photostat. Even a recording. They could turn every nation in the world against us."

"But nothing like that exists. It never has."

"Probably you're right. I'm just ticking off the possibilities. Do you think we *could* get through to President Burgess?"

"That's what I was thinking of. I bet the President would grab even the slightest bit of rationale to avoid going through with the Talbott Agreement plan. I think we have to provide him with it, give him a reason to at least reconsider it, and get the Joint Chiefs to calm down."

"I'll have to rely on your judgment," Chang said. "I know more about Red China than about the Pentagon. Think we can reach him?"

"Not by ourselves. If we get to Stephenson first, maybe we can set up some sort of meeting and lay it on the line. Once he sees what you can do with this PK thing, he'll *have* to believe there's a new twist to the imbalance of power."

Chang sat back in his chair. "I don't even know if Stephenson would listen to us. Seemed to me he's pretty much allied with Galanaugh and the Joint Chiefs, and those bastards are hotter than hell about this 'Agreement.' It's their goddamn orgasm."

"I know that. They'd put it in effect tomorrow, if they were allowed to. They think they're going in to zap the Red Chinese, and divide up the country in a matter of days. They don't realize the defense capabilities the Chinese have now to slow down the operation, and make a major nuclear war out of it. God *damn* it! I can't believe we're the only ones who realize it."

Chang frowned. "Sure, I agree with you, but how the hell do we talk them out of it?"

"I say we just lay it on the line to him how Red China could turn the Talbott Agreement plan into an all-out war. Get him to realize that if we eliminate Red China's PK abilities, then we still have a decent military superiority. And if we, say, let them into the United Nations— hell, they'd be forced to start negotiating about nuclear armament. It's working with Russia, isn't it?"

"But we've been against the U.N. admission all along."

"We can't hold out forever. It's going to happen, so why not let it happen *now*, while we still have the stronger position? Hell, they'd never get *anything* settled if Red China sat down as cocksure of themselves as they would with their PK ability."

Chang said nothing for a long time, while Moser picked up his apple again and finished it. Then Chang turned to Moser.

"Jim," he said, nearly whispering, "you said 'eliminate' China's PK ability. Are you thinking what I'm thinking?"

Moser nodded slowly. "And you can't talk me out of it. We're *both* going in."

Chang turned toward the window. Then the airman second class came out of the cockpit, holding a yellow slip of paper. He walked directly to Moser and handed it to him.

"This just came in, Captain. It's a special message for you."

Moser took the paper and unfolded it. The staccato lines of capital letters met his eyes:

REPORT DIRECTLY TO MY OFFICE IMMED ON ARRIVAL . . . ESCORT WILL MEET YOUR PLANE AT ANDREWS AFB . . . BERNADETTE TALBOTT MISSING

STEPHENSON

CHAPTER SEVEN

Among the crowd gathered noisily around the Delta Airlines' baggage recovery area at Miami International Airport was a tall but inconspicuous Oriental in an olive Palm Beach suit and white Panama hat. As the carousel began to turn and the crowd edged closer to its rim, every pair of eyes darting from suitcase to suitcase as they followed the luggage around the complete circle, the Oriental simply reached between two priests and removed his small leather overnight bag. He turned, slowly, and strolled through the terminal.

He located the rent-a-car counter, put down the case, and ordered a Mustang. The crimson-jacketed girl behind the counter efficiently signed him in, filling out the forms. "Where can you be reached, sir?" she asked.

"I don't know yet," the man said. "I'll be in Miami Beach somewhere."

"You have no telephone or hotel accommodations yet?"

"No."

"We should have a contact number, sir. If you can, would you please call this desk as soon as you know where you'll be staying?"

The man agreed, and the girl asked for his driver's license. He produced it quickly, smiling at her. Then she handed him the keys and he walked to the parking lot, reaching for his sunglasses.

He drove northward on the parkway, in the opposite direction from Miami Beach. Traffic was light on the tree-lined road. He had never been in the tropics, but the lush green vegetation and coconut trees reminded him of films of South America he'd seen once, when he was younger. Now he was one of the most trusted and efficient interrogators working for the United Front Workers Department in the United States. He was on his way to prepare for his latest—and perhaps most enjoyable—assignment. He had received word from K'ang Sheng himself that the network of United Front Workers in this country had at last tracked down the individual who seemed most likely to be persuaded to reveal the details of the new Talbott Agreement. He was to extract either a confession of guilt, together with the details, or photographic proof that the Agreement existed—either or both of these from someone he knew only as a pretty redhead named Bernadette Talbott. He stepped on the gas, anxious to reach the bait shop and make preparations. He touched the grained leather case on the seat beside him and smiled again. It contained specially devised instruments, the tool-kit of his trade.

He swerved off the throughway and paid his toll. He was in Boca Raton, a favorite coastal fishing resort for the Miami and West Palm Beach set. Masts and sails and white hulls crisscrossed against the sky and bay, a sea-collage at the foot of the picturesque village. Looking for a motel, he turned townward, and stopped at the largest he could find, parking his car in the rear of the lot, and registering under the name of Edmond Tom. He went directly to his room and called for a cab. When it arrived, he told the driver to take him to Pier 43.

He watched from the window of the taxi as the scenery flashed by—small cafes dotting the walkways like Lego cubes, children running about in bare feet and shorts, men in dungarees working on their fishing gear or scraping away on the decks and hulls of their boats. He smiled; the aura of tranquility amused him.

At a long-planked walk, he got out of the cab and strolled toward a small shop at the end. It had a ramshackle roof, covered with corrugated tin, and its walls were scabbed with blistering paint. The sign over the door read: "LEE'S BAIT & TACKLE. Chin Lee, Prop."

The man stepped up his pace and approached the shack. He hesitated briefly at the door, his hand on the rusty latch. Then he took a deep breath and, hefting his overnight case, went inside.

The pungent odors of the shop disgusted him. He thought of sour bars in New York where he'd had to make intelligence contacts and mail drops. This smelled worse than the worst of the Manhattan dives. There were fishing rods and enormous marlin hooks hanging everywhere, and innumerable tanks of live fish and bait. Behind a counter sat a squat Chinese in a wine-stained tee shirt. He was reading a Chinese newspaper, and was surprised when the well-dressed man entered.

In careful Cantonese, the visitor asked the coded question.

The fat Chinese remained cautious and impassive as he stared at the taller man. He asked the customer, "Where do you live, sir?"

The taller man replied, "The Great Proletarian Cultural Revolution will prevail."

With that, the squat baitman lifted his hulk from the chair and walked unsurely around the counter. He nodded obediently to the authoritative stranger before him. "Arrangements have been made, sir. You will work in the back of the shop this evening."

*   *   *

Bernadette's day had been pleasant. Knowing that an afternoon *Allianza* meeting would keep her at Walker's Cay, she decided to indulge herself and sleep in. She awoke to find her body lethargic, but her usually ordered mind was dancing and tumbling over random snatches of the previous evening. She hugged a pillow to her cheek and giggled into it as she thought of last night's swim. Then she remembered that Jim Moser was already gone, and she slid out of bed, briefly subdued, but the face that looked back from her mirror glowed happily. "You're shameless!" she told her dimpling image.

She had coffee sent up, then showered, bringing her bounding thoughts under control in the refreshing pinpoints of water. She dressed carefully for her 2 P.M. meeting, and went down for a late lunch. Her papers and presentation were already in order, and after repairing her makeup, she sat at one end of the veranda, making an attempt to read further in Toynbee's latest treatise.

This particular *Allianza* meeting was brief, concerned only with a final presentation of facts already considered, and a polling of the members or representatives present. It was soon over, and Bernadette returned to her room to collect her belongings. She was an experienced traveler, and packed her case quickly and efficiently, asking the steward to send it to the launch before sailing time.

Bernadette had agreed to an early dinner engagement, and it was convivial, with two attractive men as companions, Martin Peterson, of the World Bank, and General Raul Sarmiento, of Peru. The General was older, a romantic Latin with insinuating eyes, she thought. Peterson was something else; tall and thin, and completely bald, he had a golden tongue, and a prodigious memory for almost anything, it seemed. But the pleasant evening escaped them, and soon she and Peterson were waving to the General as he boarded a seaplane to make connections to South America.

Now, in the twilight, Bernadette Talbott stepped gingerly into the small launch and turned to wave goodbye to Martin Peterson, whose head gleamed through the dusk. Captain Sam Goffredo, of the Coast Guard, held her arm, steadying her and helping her over the gunwale. He would be her escort on the late evening flight from Miami back to Washington, and she followed him now as he took her luggage into the shelf-lined compartment. "You'll like the skipper," he said. "His name is Sims. He's a retired Army colonel who owns this and helps us out when we don't want to transport people in military vessels."

Inside, Sims' face crinkled into a smile. "Best looking cargo the 'Bahamian Queen' ever had."

"Sorry I'm overdressed for the occasion," she said.

"Not a bit." Sims' eyes twinkled, as he started the engine, and the boat began to slide through the twilight bay.

It was thirty miles from Walker's Cay to Miami— about two and a half hours for the little launch. Bernadette relaxed and listened as Sims spilled out anecdotes about his new life. He was a quiet, witty man who had doffed his Army career with his uniform. Now the sea salted his speech, the new-found joys of an uncomplicated boatsman's world smiled through his eyes. Bernadette tried to imagine him, stiff and official, reviewing the regiment in his colonel's uniform. That man was the phony, she guessed to herself. This is the real Sims.

She sat next to his pilot's seat on a wooden bench, across from Goffredo. She had taken off her shoes, and now had a pink sweater pulled over her shoulders. The night was balmy. She was enjoying the two men's company and the droning throb of the engine as they thrashed through the water. The bow splashed against wave after wave with an intricate Latin rhythm that lent a movie-score background to the soft tropic night.

Sims was looking at the compass, then at Bernadette, then peering into the darkness outside. "Things sure have changed," he muttered. "Yes, ma'am. When I got out of the Army, I swore I wouldn't do any more work for them. We always did hate these Seabee types."

Goffredo smiled good naturedly. "Look who's a Seabee now."

Sims shrugged. "Well, after all, you guys pay me pretty good for these special trips. They got a lot of dough now, ma'am, not like while I was in. The Army always got the short end of things, anyway. By the way, if you're hungry, there's some fresh shrimp and some cold beer in the ice box."

Bernadette shook her head. Goffredo got up and walked to the window. "Are there usually many craft out at this hour?"

"No, not around here. Oh, maybe a late returning trawler or two. Sometimes we see some Russian trawlers, but it's been a long time since they've been around. Snooping around the Cape, I'd say."

"I think there's something out there," Goffredo said. He looked out again. "Someone's approaching us. Better put the running lights on."

Sims looked out and saw a flashing white lamp.

"They're signaling us. Looks like they might be in trouble, whoever they are." He reached down for the throttle and cut the engine back. At the same time, he turned off the cabin lights and switched on the red and white running lights.

Fifty yards away, the dark form of a trawler loomed in a black-on-black mosaic of stars and shadows. A single beacon pulsed at them. Sims studied the pulses. I-N-J-U-R-Y O-N B-O-A-R-D N-E-E-D A-I-D. Sims turned to Goffredo. "Shall we stop?"

"Goddamn it all! Switch on the searchlight and take a look at who they are."

Bernadette pressed her face against the cold pane of glass. She kept silent. They saw a grey and blue fishing vessel with a single, dim yellow light in its cabin. Two men were silhouetted in front of it, one motioning to them.

"They want us to heave to and help," Sims said, turning to Goffredo.

"Well, let's take a look."

Sims guided the launch toward the other boat. He approached from the starboard side. Both Sims and Goffredo went out on the bridge. A voice, in a Cuban accent, called from the darkness. "We have an injured man and no medical kit. Can you take him on board?"

Goffredo cupped his mouth and yelled, "We'll give you our kit. Heave alongside."

In another minute, the boat was next to them, and as Goffredo started to throw the small tin box to the other man, five figures emerged with rifles and machine guns. They leveled them at the two. A husky voice, different from the other, called out in a heavy accent. "Both of you stay where you are. We're coming aboard."

The five armed men boarded the launch. "Where is the woman?"

Inside the cabin, Bernadette began to panic.

Goffredo and Sims raised their hands. "We are American citizens," Goffredo said curtly. "I am an American officer."

The leader said nothing and gestured to the others. He

spoke in Spanish as two men entered the cabin. Sims and Goffredo stood helpless as they emerged with Bernadette between them, each holding one of her wrists. They took her to the side of the boat. A third man joined them as they shoved her across the black water onto the ship. She screamed and stumbled, falling on the deck. Two men grabbed her and dragged her below where they threw her onto a bunk. Her hands were tied behind her. The two men leered at her and chattered in slurred Spanish. Then they left her in the darkness. Bernadette heard the bolt of the door snap in its latch. The excited voices were muffled through the bulkhead. She thought she heard Sims yelling, but the sound was chopped by the ear-splitting clatter of machine-gun fire. She began to cry as she heard the rumble of the engines beneath her, and felt the boat surge through the water.

*   *   *

The wet nylon ropes were cutting into her wrists, but Bernadette had stopped struggling long ago. It only made them hurt more. She sat, tied to a straight-back bamboo chair, facing a dilapidated bed against the wall of a closed room. The bed was rusty, and its rotting mattress smelled of urine. There was no sound except the creaking of the piles, and she guessed an attempt had been made to soundproof the room. There was no window, but she judged it must be well into the morning. A single dim bulb in the corner made half-silhouettes of everything. The shadows were broken periodically by a moth darting with incessant furor into the light.

Her shoes had fallen off when she was carried into the room, but the thin pink sweater still clung to her shoulders. Both her stockings had runs in them, and her dress was matted with grease. Her hair was wet and ragged, clinging to the back of her neck. Her lipstick had long been bitten off. She was hungry, and even the odious smell of old fish tantalized her.

She tried to think. The launch had been sunk by the unmarked boat. They had tied her and carried her into the dirty ship, and she hadn't seen another person since. Only voices. Somehow she suspected a connection with

Chang. But what? She had no way of knowing where she was; they had blindfolded her during the transfer from the boat to this place. She had no way of knowing who or what organization had kidnapped her. It was probably Cuban. She thought of Jim, and wondered if they had him, too. If they did, was he here? Where *was* she? A fishing village somewhere, she could tell. Cuba? No, the boat trip was not that long. In Florida? Perhaps in some remote island in the Florida Keys?

And why? Who was doing this? The Red Chinese?

Fears and speculations continued to vault and somersault through her mind. Who could know that I was even going to that meeting?

Escape was out of the question. She was bound securely by the wrists and ankles. The door was surely locked. Besides, she didn't have the strength. She doubted if she could even stand up.

Her thoughts were suddenly cut off by a creaking at the door. It opened, and a tall Chinese stepped into the room. He walked over and stood behind her. He, too, cast grotesque shadows on the bare walls. In the doorway, outlined by the bare bulb, Chin Lee peered in gleefully. His mouth was moist with cheap rum, and he gave her a toothless leer.

She was revolted, and stared resolutely back at the pudgy Chinese, saying nothing.

The voice behind her was polite. "Miss Talbott, I have to apologize for your rough treatment. Are your bonds too tight?"

"What do you intend to do with me?" Her voice dripped with anger.

The voice was distant and passive, almost mechanical in its condescending monotone. "We plan you no harm, Miss Talbott. That is, if you cooperate with us."

Bernadette shuddered.

"Is there anything I can get you, Miss Talbott?"

"Water."

He motioned to the figure in the doorway, and the fat man staggered away and returned to hand her a soiled glass of tepid water. He held it to her lips and she could smell the grimy sweat on the back of his hand as she gagged the water down. He left. Then the voice from behind her spoke again. "What would entice you to return to the Chinese mainland with me, Miss Talbott?"

"That's ridiculous, and you know it."

"Perhaps not. I'm prepared to offer you five hundred thousand American dollars if you return to China with me."

"Five hundred thousand! You're insane! What good would that do me in that sick country of yours? Who *are* you?"

"Let's just say I'm a friend of the Chinese people. We have our CIA, too, Miss Talbott. My government knows you are aware of the details of the agreement that bears your name."

Bernadette pressed her lips together. She decided to bide her time. Wait for an opening.

"It would make you a very rich woman, Miss Talbott. You'd be a virtual princess and receive the greatest respect in the highest social circles. I can promise you that."

"That's absurd," she snapped defiantly.

"Miss Talbott," the voice was still soft, but she noted a slight change in timbre. "Please be reasonable. I assure you that it is in your best interests. We intend to call this monstrous plan to the attention of the entire world to eliminate any plans you and the Soviet Union have. Of course, we need the proof. We are asking you to confess your crime and attest to the validity of what your government and the Soviets intend to do."

Bernadette's fears rose. Now she knew the implications of Chang's statements at Walker's Cay. "I won't do it, of course," she said.

"You will." The voice rose in pitch. "What remains to be seen is whether you choose to live in my country as a princess or as a prisoner. You have that choice, Miss Talbott. You alone."

"You'll never make it back to Red China. As soon as they find the launch didn't return to Miami, which I'm sure they already have, they'll track you down and kill you. You don't have a chance in the world to return to Red China."

"You underestimate me," he continued. "I have my orders to extract a confession from you at all costs. I have been in the service of my government too long to fail."

"I will do nothing to help you." Bernadette heard her voice falter. She could feel the man behind her smile.

"You will, of course," he said. "We have persuaded information from Cuban exiles many times, and I assure you, we have developed some very persuasive techniques. Some unique."

Bernadette's eyes grew turgid. She tensed against her bonds. No, it was useless.

"I am trying to be reasonable, Miss Talbott. But if you won't sign a confession, I will be forced to introduce you to Mr. Lee outside. He is much more, shall we say, *physical* than I. Time grows short, Miss Talbott. I have to signal the trawler and leave shortly. Once again, I ask for your cooperation."

"No," she said, her voice quavering. "I will not cooperate."

"I'm disappointed. A woman as brilliant as you. A woman with perception and an active mind. You must consider the alternatives. You recognize, of course, that you are not, *not,* in a bargaining position. I'm afraid your signature will be physically forced from you."

She heard the man turn and stride across the room. Bernadette sat frozen to her chair, her damp dress clinging to her and her hands shaking uncontrollably. Her eyes darted about the room, looking for openings, weapons, anything to ward off the horrid fat man she knew would enter at any moment.

That moment came quickly. A pale, bloated face was leering at her. Chin Lee closed the door behind him. His right hand still held the bottle of rum. He put it to his lips and drank a large gulp. Then he wiped his lips with his sleeve, and set the bottle on the floor. Without saying a word and with surprisingly gentle hands, he taped Bernadette's mouth with a wide piece of adhesive cloth.

Then, after another gulp from the bottle, he leaned toward her.

He whirled sharply, and slapped her hard across the mouth. The force of the blow spun her head and she felt the sting on her reddening cheek. Then, still smiling, he hit her again on the other cheek, toppling her over. She winced as her shoulder hit the floor.

Chin Lee righted the chair and Bernadette together. He noticed that her dress had crept up over the tops of her stockings. With a detached curiosity, he pulled up her skirt around her waist and tore her stockings down. Then he began whipping her thighs with a fiberglass fishing pole. Sharp, stinging blows cut into her flesh. She began to bleed.

Bernadette had never experienced such pain. Her mind reeled and her legs grew numb. She looked at herself, at the bloody stripes tingling in hot, searing pulses.

Chin Lee stood back and looked clinically at his subject. He was a hazy blur through her tears.

He approached her again. He removed the pink sweater from her shoulders, and carefully unbuttoned the front of her dress. He drew it down. Then he reached out, grabbing at her bra, yanking it off. He grinned as he noted the breasts, and the delicate rosy nipples.

Then Chin Lee reached for a can of fish hooks.

*   *   *

Stephenson filled his pipe and lit it with a kitchen match. He glared across the desk at Moser. "It's all right with me. Hell, I don't give a damn."

"I'd like to go. And I think it would do her good to see me."

"We should have closed that Boca Raton exit *years* ago. But we had no idea this would happen. At any rate, apparently Bernadette did sign a confession, and that puts us in a hell of a fix. Whoever it was was an operative who flew in from New York especially for the assignment. As far as we can ascertain, he rented a car and registered at a motel under the name of Edmond Tom. He then took a cab directly to Lee's Bait Shop. A Cuban fishing boat probably picked her up. We spotted a trawler in the area but it got back to Cuba. So we're out of luck there. Bernadette didn't remember how much she told them."

"Has the President been told yet?"

"No, not about Bernadette. We thought it best to wait until we have the report in full. He has been briefed on the intelligence Chang brought us. Tomorrow morning he'll discuss it with both you and Chang. A little different from teaching, isn't it, Captain?"

Moser didn't smile.

* * *

Moser was out of the seaplane almost before it had fully stopped. In another minute he was leaping from the small boat onto the boardwalk. A CIA man stepped from a black car and intercepted him.

"Alan Jackson, CIA, Captain. I was told to meet you. We're to head right for the hospital."

Moser asked the question again. "How bad is she?"

"Not as bad as it looked when we first found her. Severe lacerations on her upper thighs, mostly superficial. Must have hurt, but no damage. Some welts. Lost very little blood. Worst thing is they tried to mutilate her breasts."

Moser's stomach began to turn. He felt sick. Rage churned within him, frothing and bubbling like peroxide on an open sore. "What else?" he forced himself to say.

"That's all. They probably would have killed her—or they may have thought she was dead already. As soon as we got word, we figured she might have been brought to that contact point. We've known about it for some time, and let it operate so we could keep an eye on them. But we didn't have any agents in the area at the time, so we called the local police. They must have made quite a commotion getting in, because the agent we were after got away. The other one, Chin Lee, was the regular contact for the Cuban exit. We found him with a marlin hook through his neck. But the papers Miss Talbott signed—gone. Probably in Cuba by now. We're shit out of luck."

The two men got into the car and drove off. Moser was quiet, almost sullen, and Jackson drove carefully, expertly, his face expressionless and clinical in professional demeanor.

*   *   *

In a small hospital in nearby Simpson Beach, Bernadette was finishing a cup of broth, toast, and a glass of tomato juice. She passed over the coffee on the small tray, and asked the matronly nurse whether there was any other kind of juice.

"Orange and tomato. That's all, I'm afraid."

"Am I allowed to have a large glass of ice-cold milk?"

"I'll have to check with the doctor," the nurse said. Bernadette sighed in irritation. "It's *just* milk, nurse. I'm terribly thirsty."

The nurse shrugged her shoulders. "I don't make the rules around here, miss. I just follow orders. I'll ask the doctor if you can have some." She exited in a flurry of white.

Bernadette turned on the radio near the bed, and waited. She looked at the unfinished glass of juice. Her breasts tingled with sharp, stinging pain when she moved, and the hospital gown rubbed abrasively through her bandages. Her thighs were sore, too, and on her cheeks were bruises where he had hit her. She looked in the small bedside mirror and retouched her makeup. Her hair was combed, at last, and she began to feel like a woman again, except for the pain. A smaller, prettier nurse brought in a large glass of milk, and Bernadette gulped it down quickly, asking immediately for a second.

"Another one?"

She nodded patiently. "Builds strong bones," she said. Then she lay back and tried to relax. The door opened and the nurse came in with another glass of milk. Behind her was Jim Moser.

"Jim!" Bernadette sat up quickly. The nurse put the milk down, and left the room, smiling, and closing the door. Without speaking, and with a grim expression on his face, Moser stepped to the bed and buried his face in her neck. She wrapped her arms around him, wincing slightly, and whispered into his ear as she kissed him. "Oh, Jim," and tears filled her eyes as she clung to him.

"I got here as soon as I could," Moser said in a low tone. "I . . . I'm sorry, Bernie. How're you doing?"

"I was lucky," she said, smiling at him and wiping at her tears with the back of her hand, child-fashion. "I'm not as bad off as I could be, according to the doctor. I'll be out of here soon, don't worry."

He sat down on the bed and held her hands. He saw her face, the bluish bruises worse on her right cheek, but otherwise there was no visible change. "I heard what they did," he said. "Christ!"

"It's all right. I'll be fine. How about handing me a cigarette? They're in that drawer over there."

Moser got up and returned with cigarettes and matches. He lit one for her.

"Did they tell you I signed a confession? I'm sorry. I couldn't stand it. He brought out a kit of tools, and . . ."

Bernadette turned her head away. Her nerves were still raw, and tears slid silently down her cheeks. She dabbed them quickly away and brought herself into check. "He first tried to talk me into returning to the Chinese mainland with him. I guess if I wanted to avoid all the rest of it, I could have agreed to it and just tried to escape somehow."

Moser looked at her and his concerned eyes continued to scan her marked face.

"I passed out, or something, but I don't remember whether I said anything later on. I do remember holding a pen though, and someone taking a picture of me. I don't know where or how they're going to use those pictures. I looked like I'd been through hell. So it'll be quite a touch-up job." She smiled at him. "I didn't even have my lipstick on."

Moser finally grinned at her. "You're too much," he said, taking her hands and sliding further up on the bed. "They almost kill you, and you're worried about how you looked." Then he added, "Pretty bad, huh, Bernie?"

She sighed. "I thought so. They tried out some new

ones on me, I'll say that. I guess my legs and breasts are the worst. The next time you see me in a bathing suit I'll look like a master sergeant or something."

"Scars?"

"I'm only kidding. They say no scars, and that I'll be out of here in a day or so."

"Listen, why don't you stay at my place when you get back? Just lie around and rest. Listen to music, drink beer, that sort of thing."

"I'd love to," she said. "But I may not be in any shape for a while, if you're planning on going for a swim."

"I'll live. Chang and I are seeing the President as soon as I get back. We hope to convince him to let us get Tsien out, so he can announce a pro U.N. vote and force them to the table. Without Tsien, they'll be scared silly of Russia and us."

"I'm not sure I go along with that. The Talbott Agreement is the only thing that can keep them from throwing nuclear bombs at us in a few years."

Moser shook his head. "No, once we get them to the table we can start controlling them. Look at us and Russia . . . we're even inspecting each other's nuclear sites now."

"China won't agree to that."

"Not even if we have everyone else in the world staring down their throats in the General Assembly?"

"I don't know," she said. She sighed. "I'm not for killing people, you know. But I just don't have much sense of security for the free world when I think of what Mao Tse-tung's been saying. Then they start testing nuclear weapons long before we even thought they'd *have* them. You've got to admit, it's pretty frightening."

"It's *because* it's so frightening, Bernie, that we've got to find another solution besides all-out warfare. It doesn't make sense to start a war in order to prevent one, does it? And you can bet, since Chang's new information, that they'll be pretty well able to ball up our attack to the point where it'll last a while."

She looked out the window and hummed the tune that was playing on the radio.

CHAPTER EIGHT

The President of the United States, John Robert Burgess, had only been in office seven months. He was a fast-moving man who had appointed an entire new cabinet just a month after his election. The men he chose reflected his own dynamism; men who digested facts and who cut through to the core of a problem, who boiled events down to their barest essential significance, and then made a decision.

Burgess won the election by a slim majority, but he wasn't one to walk on eggshells for lack of a political mandate. He was now the President, and he was his own man with his own policies. A former senator from Pennsylvania, and a former mayor of Pittsburgh, Burgess was a political pragmatist. He had been through the smoky rooms, the vote-getting maneuverings at Harrisburg, the endless hundred-dollar creamed-chicken dinners, and at this stage of his life based his decisions on his own convictions rather than political favoritism, on morality and reality rather than compromise and partisanism. Already, Burgess was either liked or disliked—no wait-and-see shades of grey—and the American people had indicated they would trust his benevolent father-image candor rather than the bombast of his millionaire conservative opponent. The latest Gallup poll indicated that, as of a week ago, the election would have been a landslide in his favor rather than the threadlike 53 per cent majority.

Burgess was fifty-seven, with ample locks of curly white hair. His gnarled features contrasted with the friendly wrinkles about his eyes and mouth; the eyes were blue, the eyebrows thick, bushy, and white. He had a boisterous but infectious laugh, one which worked in his favor when asked a witty question at his weekly television press conferences.

His wife had died three years before the election, a cancer victim, and now his oldest daughter, Jennifer, saw to what would normally be the First Lady's White House decorating responsibilities. She'd done the many rooms of the building in a more contemporary style than Burgess would have preferred, but he had given her full reign, and refrained from adverse comments. His other daughter was a senior in college.

Burgess's directness since the inauguration had, on several occasions, caused great glee among the quote-hungry Washington press corps. His irritation and disgust with many of the errors he had inherited were voiced, and not couched in political ambiguities, for he was faced with stemming a tide of skepticism and apathy.

As he looked across his desk at his four visitors, his jaw was set and his lips were drawn tight. Moser noted how he fiddled with a gold pencil and doodled endless circles and arrows on the pad of white paper before him. Moser liked him instantly. The President's handshake was firm and friendly—no doubt conditioned by the years of campaigning—and his gait was confident and sure. His voice was gentle, yet persuasive, and made those with him feel at ease quickly. Beside the desk lay a husky German shepherd named George.

Next to Moser sat Chang Kwok-wah, in a blue business suit. Facing the President, from the other side of the oval room, were Lawrence Golding, the Secretary of Defense, and Stephenson. Behind them the French doors opened onto the rear garden of the White House.

"You've led a pretty interesting life, Mr. Chang," the President said, putting down the pencil and intertwining his fingers as he set his hands firmly on the desk. "I read your dossier last night. You've taken quite a few risks for your country."

"Thank you, sir," Chang said politely. "I hope it will prove rewarding to the country. My training by Captain Moser here had a lot to do with it."

The President looked at Moser, nodded, and returned his glance to Chang. "I know," he said. "Are you married?"

Chang hesitated. "No, sir. I'm not."

The President grinned wryly. "Thought you may have met a pretty Communist over there. There *are* such things, I hear."

Chang returned the grin. "Many of them. But a lot of bad-looking ones, too."

The President tapped his hands on the desk. "I'll spare you the old joke, Mr. Chang. I know you've heard it too many times before."

Chang smiled again, appreciating the man's warmth and obvious respect for the Oriental's background.

"What bothers me most about this thing, I think," the President then said seriously, "is how they got the information about this damn Talbott Agreement. Have you any idea?"

Chang shrugged. "No, sir. They got their hint about it from a coded radio link from North Korea through Japan. Under K'ang Sheng, as you probably know, the United Front Workers Department has spread itself all over the place. Who knows exactly where the Talbott Agreement intelligence was cranked in?"

The President looked at Stephenson. "I want that leak tracked down, Tony." Stephenson nodded, knowing excuses were to no avail. It was all the President had to say.

Then the President looked at Moser. "I understand you interviewed Bernadette Talbott, Captain. How much did she tell them?"

Moser suppressed his nervousness, and leaned forward in his chair, elbows resting on the cushioned arms. "She's not sure, sir. She was drugged or something after she wouldn't talk, but she vaguely remembers holding a pencil and their taking photographs."

"If you had to make an assumption, what would it be?"

"I'd be forced to assume the Communists now at least know the general scope of the Agreement, sir."

"I understand she was tortured."

"Yes, sir."

"Badly?"

"Yes, sir."

The President shook his head and frowned. The idea was distasteful to him. "What about the agent?" he asked Stephenson.

"Got away. Probably to Cuba. We found an oil slick and debris in the vicinity of a sub we've been tracking, and saw a civilian on it in Havana when it refueled. We think he rendezvoused with the sub, destroying whatever small craft he went out in."

The President stood up abruptly and moved in long strides behind his desk as he began to pace back and forth. "I don't like this whole setup, gentlemen, as at least one of you already knows. I was appalled when I was first apprised of it last December during my transition session. Now, what I want to know are your suggestions for which way to go on this. Tony?"

Stephenson looked briefly at Secretary Golding, then back to the President. "Mr. Chang and Captain Moser here have a rather drastic but workable plan, Mr. President. They've been hoping your position would be similar to what you've just indicated."

The President allowed a brief grin. "I'm not too hard to predict, they say. Captain Moser, what have you got in mind?"

Moser leaned forward again. "Sir, Chang and I both believe, after giving it some hard and authoritative thought, that we can convince Dr. Tsien to repatriate to America. It would be tough, but Chang still has his cover and is very close to Tsien. He and I would go back into China and bring Tsien out."

The President was visibly intrigued. "I've read his dossier, too, Captain, and it would seem highly improbable after the treatment we gave him. I remember that investigating committee."

Chang spoke. "Mr. President, I have worked with Dr. Tsien for five years, and he has come to trust me as his most valuable assistant. He's a kind and gentle man, but admittedly bitter. He's highly respected among the Chinese hierarchy and has carte blanche to do what he wants. His leaving would be extremely simple, once we talked him into it. And I'm sure he'd listen to me when I describe the Talbott Agreement to him in detail."

"If you did convince him, how would you and Moser get out?"

Chang looked at Moser. "We'd have to figure that out, too. Rely on another operative's coordination."

"And you think Tsien's leaving would get us out of all this?"

Moser spoke up, getting more passionate in his inflections. "Mr. President, without Tsien the Chinese would have no defense against the Talbott Agreement. Right now, when they hear about it, they'll only shrug it off, knowing full well they'd have an upper hand with Tsien's psychokinesis techniques. But without him, they'd have to force us to drop the plan, or else agree to sit down and discuss the nuclear question. It would give us some *time*, sir. Time to figure out another way to prevent a nuclear war originating in Red China."

The President sat down heavily and rubbed his eyes with his thick palms. "You're not very sympathetic with this plan, are you, Captain?" he said without looking up.

"No, sir, we're not. Not at all," Moser said.

The President looked up once more and his eyes were red where he had rubbed them hard with his hands. He sighed.

"We think," Moser said, hoping the President would appreciate frankness, "that it's been blown out of proportion by the Joint Chiefs and by the Soviets' insistence on it."

The President leaned back and lit a cigarette. He looked at the smoke curling from it, glanced at the ceiling, and then looked around the room. Then he leaned forward and picked up a flat gold plate, which lay near his bank of official law-signing pens. "I want all of you to read this before I state my own idea on this thing. I think we have the seed of something here, and I want all of you to know my own thoughts on why we may very well pro-

ceed in this direction." As he handed the plate first to
Moser, he added, "There are a lot of politicians around
who'd be pretty damn surprised to know I've read any
Santayana."

Moser accepted the plate and read an engraved inscription on its polished surface:

Where parties and governments are bad, as they are in
most ages and countries, it makes practically no differ-
ence to a community, apart from local ravages, whether
its own army or the enemy's is victorious in war. . . .
The private citizen in any event continues in such countries to pay a maximum of taxes and to suffer, in all his
private interests, a maximum of vexation and neglect.
Nevertheless . . . the oppressed subject will glow like the
rest with patriotic ardor, and will decry as dead to duty
and honor anyone who points out as perverse this helpless allegiance to a government representing no public interest.

                                    George Santayana
                                    Reason In Society

Moser smiled as he finished reading the plate, and
passed it to Chang. His glance made Chang begin reading
immediately. By the time everyone had finished, with the
President watching each person for facial reaction, the
room was silent, except for the snip-snip of pruning
shears from beyond the French doors, where a gardener
puttered among the many rose bushes.

Then the President spoke, and there was a new tone to
his voice, a more vigorous passion, a renewed fervor.

"It's been a growing fear with me, gentlemen, that
we're rapidly becoming a government with no public interest, a government that merely makes the public *believe*
we have an interest in it, but which actually doesn't give a
damn about the individual. I think we are doing exactly
what Santayana has said such a government does. We are
producing a maximum of vexation and neglect for the
private citizen. We spend millions on helping the under-

privileged, the minorities, the urban slums. Yet the money is barely worth anything by the time it gets down to them. We spend billions to get to the moon, when the private citizen actually doesn't give a damn whether we get there or not, and has no tangible evidence of what it will mean to him when and if we do. We spend billions in armament, in nuclear weapons and missiles, and tell him it's for his security, while we send his son off to get a pungi stick in his balls."

Moser decided that if he was still alive in 1972, he would vote for this man and actively campaign for him.

"In short, I agree that no one wins a war when it is fought between such governments, and if we descend to the depths the Chinese Communists want us to, indeed we will be one of those governments. Because of that, I'd like us to be very frank with each other."

He drew a deep breath again and leaned back, hands outstretched to the tips of the arms of his mahogany chair. "I was elected because the people of this country are sick of the military running the country. They're sick of seeing their own cities burning, their own neighborhoods being ransacked, and their wives raped in the streets while we spend billions of dollars being the world's policeman. When I saw the details of the Talbott Agreement, I was sickened. When I saw the gleeful looks on the faces of our generals, I was disgusted. That is why I've called a moratorium on the planning of Phase Three of the agreement. Naturally, that annoyed our problem child, didn't it, Larry?" The President smiled and looked at the Secretary of Defense, who smiled back at the reference to General Galanaugh. Moser felt his new enthusiasm growing. He shared the President's apparent distaste for Galanaugh's attitudes.

"Now, personally," Burgess went on, "Galanaugh is a pretty warm human being. I've been to dinner with him, chatted with him many times since taking office. He's knowledgeable and capable, and actually, in himself, isn't the real problem. The problem is that we've lived with the military—with military action, if you please—for so long that these men know no other solutions to the world's problems. To them, military action is a way of life, the only solution to getting people to agree with our own democratic philosophies." He smiled at Moser. "No reflection on you, Captain."

Moser smiled back, caught up in the momentum of the conversation. "I haven't been in any action since mock field exercises at Little Shanghai, sir. But does this mean you're considering our proposal?"

The President nodded. "I still have to be convinced that bringing Tsien out will provide a workable method of cancelling the Talbott Agreement."

"Well," Moser said, seizing another opportunity, "I'm sure you're aware of the DEIMOS project out at Seneca Corporation. Chang blew it sky high. He proved China is way ahead of us in this ability. By 1972 it can be effectively used against the Talbott Agreement. China would be free to counterattack without interference—and even their limited striking power could do a lot of damage. The only way to prevent the Talbot Agreement from becoming a deadly, prolonged nuclear conflict is to get Dr. Tsien out and neutralize Red China's PK capability, sir."

"And how do you propose we get rid of the Agreement altogether?" the President asked.

Moser answered quickly. "We think the Red Chinese won't disclose the Talbott Agreement to the world at large for some time. They'll wait to get maximum diplomatic advantage. Without their PK capability, they'll be afraid enough of the Agreement to sit down, finally, and talk about some sort of nuclear missile controls."

Burgess eyed Moser. "I think I already know what you're going to say, Captain, but exactly how and where do we sit down and talk about this?"

Moser hesitated momentarily, then went on. "In the United Nations, sir. If we announce that we've decided to let them in, it will take all the credibility out of their Talbott Agreement announcement, and it will give us a chance to eliminate the Agreement altogether and open the way to more peaceful methods of controlling the nuclear powers."

The President's eyes lit up. "That's very interesting,"

he mused. "And what about Russia? They'll be hopping mad when we withdraw from the Agreement."

"We'll have to take our chances on that, sir. Chang and I agree that they'll have no choice but to continue to honor our own nuclear agreements, such as Operation Tonsillectomy, and go along with the U.N. talks."

Golding sat up straight. "How do *you* know about that, Captain?"

Moser turned to Chang. "Chang has informed us that Peking already knows about it. He outlined it to us perfectly."

"Good Lord," Stephenson said. "Isn't *anything* kept secret any more?"

The President turned to him. "I guess not, when you've got thousands of agents from every country in the world spying on each other, Tony." He turned to Moser and Chang.

"I'm surprised at what you say, gentlemen. It just so happens—and this is to be held in the strictest confidence, speaking of secrets—that I intend to vote for the admission of Red China into the United Nations in three weeks, when the vote comes up again. We've privately polled many nations, and we believe we've accurately gauged the votes of the remainder, until it looks like we'll have the deciding vote. Now, from what you say, if Tsien is out and we let them into the U.N., we'll be successful, and honorably out of our Talbott Agreement commitments, right?"

"We think so. Yes, sir."

Stephenson stirred uncomfortably in his chair, and Golding crossed his legs, making notes on a small yellow pad on his lap. Outside, two men were walking casually across the rear lawn. Moser guessed they were Secret Service agents.

"And even if it turns out we *don't* have the deciding vote," the President said, "we can muster enough allies to vote with us or else persuade the abstainers to come around in our favor."

"So we're going to pull out of the Agreement and start rattling missiles with Russia again," Secretary Golding said. "That will start me and State making more motions about building up arms."

"Maybe not," Burgess said. "We seem to forget constantly that the Russians don't want a war any more than we do. They're achieving their goals quite successfully without it, and are even coming around to capitalism as a result of it. But they're scared as hell at the Chinese sitting on their doorstep and being hungry for both real estate and food. They'll come around and do whatever they can to get Red China to settle on some sort of nuclear escalation control."

Then the President stood. He faced Moser squarely. "So what we have, Captain, is a plan for you and Chang to convince Dr. Tsien to come over to our side again in order for us to rearrange things a bit. But there are two contingencies. One, I have to know within about two weeks. We can't give them any more time than that since they got to Bernadette Talbott. Two weeks. I have to know by then that you've succeeded in getting him out. Second, what happens if he doesn't agree?"

Chang spoke. "We'll have to kill him. It's the only other way to be certain this PK thing has been stopped."

The President hunched his shoulders. "I guess so," he said. "And what if you can't do that? What if . . ."

"If they get to us before we get to him?" Chang asked.

The President nodded expectantly.

"Then," Chang said, looking at Moser, "we all wait to see what happens in 1972. Whether there will be a 1973."

*   *   *

Chang went with Stephenson back to CIA headquarters for briefing on the method of entry, while Moser drove directly to his apartment. The Secretary of Defense stayed on to confer further with the President on the current Arab-Israeli outbreak of hostilities.

Moser pulled his car into the garage and got out slowly. He had been greatly encouraged by the meeting in the White House, but now his concern was growing about the forthcoming entry into Red China. It would be a lot different from either Taiwan or Korea, he thought to himself, and a helluva lot different from the Little Shanghai days. No one before had wanted to kill him, nor expose him as an American agent. Was his dialect still accurate? Could he still sing-song along in Cantonese or Mandarin without flaw, using the proper word in the proper shade of meaning, the proper inflection? And what about his mannerisms? Could he remember the little subtleties, the nuances of action and expression that conveyed so much to Orientals, but went untranslated in the Western world?

Climbing the stairs, he searched his billfold for his duplicate key. He'd given the other one to Bernadette, and he hoped she had returned by now.

" 'Home is the sailor, home from the sea,' " she quoted to him as he threw open the door.

He crossed the room and kissed her, holding her gently but firmly against him. "When did you get back?"

"About three hours ago. They sent a plane for me."

"Feel all right? How're your stripes?"

She laughed. "No bathing suits, yet. But I'm fine." She kissed him again. "If I mix the martinis, will you take me to dinner?"

"Feel up to it?" he asked, removing his tie.

She kissed him a third time. "Yes."

After dinner they drove to the Washington Monument, and Moser parked the Porsche at the end of a parking area. They strolled along the reflecting pool. A late summer moon was rising over the Capitol Building, a rusty-red, enlarged globe casting its quiet gaze over the city. They walked slowly, not speaking, but happy in each other's company. Bernadette finally spoke.

"I've made a decision today. I'm going to resign my chair at Yale."

Moser looked at her.

"I'm going to get off the podium and . . . well, let's say I'm going to take a seat in class."

"You're a little old to carry peace signs around the campus, aren't you?" he asked, smiling.

"I want to study painting and get back to the things that interested me years ago. Painting and writing. Maybe finish that novel, too. I guess I'm just tired of international affairs." She stopped. *"That* certainly didn't sound right, did it?"

Moser laughed. "I never had much interest in art, except for that corny old line about knowing what I like. Like that painting of yours I offered to buy."

"I'll do a better one for you."

"I used to like the Impressionists in college. Mostly because of those movies, I guess. *Lust for Life* and the one about Toulouse-Lautrec. What was it called?"

"Moulin Rouge," she said. "I saw it about five times. Fabulous color. I understand Houston shot it through some kind of soft-focus lens, and his composition was beautiful . . . as though Lautrec directed the film himself."

Moser shrugged. "That's what I mean. Composition, and all that, escapes me. All I know is what I like. Say, Wyeth and . . ."

"Wyeth is magnificent," she said eagerly. "I'd give anything to be able to do what he can do. I remember when I lived with my aunt, they had a whole collection of classics illustrated by his father, N. C. Wyeth. Beautiful things. Andrew works in egg tempera, one of the hardest media to use. Not much room for mistakes. They say Jamie, his son, tops the whole family."

Then she stopped for a moment, tugging at his arm. "Let's sit down over there, Jim," she said, pointing to a bench near a sprawling elm.

They sat down, and Moser carefully draped his arm around her shoulders. She wore a sweater similar to the pink one she'd had in the Bahamas.

"You can be the artistic one," Moser said, stretching his legs out straight. "But none of that crazy stuff like that gory guy. What's his name—Grotz?"

"God no," she said, grimacing. "All he does is babies bleeding and things. Warfare scenes."

At her last two words she fell into a long silence. Moser watched the moon turning slowly from orange to yellow, rising as if some slow-motion hand was in the process of balancing it atop the Washington Monument. He mentally gauged its ascending path and bet himself it wouldn't touch the tall obelisk. It would be close, though.

"Jim," she said. "Out with it."

He gave her a blank look. "With what?"

"What's going to happen? You were going to talk to the President today and you haven't said a word about it. Did he . . . ?" Her voice broke off as the tenseness in her body set off another sharp sting of pain through her breasts.

"Yes." Why talk about it, he thought. Why can't we pretend none of this is happening?

"Both of you?" His silence was answer enough. She followed his gaze up the rising moon. Her hand crept up to her shoulder, where his fingers lay stiffly. "Jim," she said after a while. "Do you *have* to go. I mean *you?*"

"I thought we discussed that already," he said evenly.

"It's just that it's so . . . so . . . un*real*. I never thought I'd get so deeply involved in this thing."

Moser didn't reply. He leaned back, removing his arm from her shoulder and threw both arms back, like a stretching cat. He bent his head far backward, then revolved his head as if trying to relax a sudden spasm in his neck. Two lovers walked past their bench, giggling—an interracial couple. Moser and Bernadette watched them as they paused and gazed up at the Monument, then down at the shimmering reflection in the pool. Then they walked on and the man said something that made his girl giggle again.

Bernadette fumbled in her purse for a cigarette. "When do you leave?" she asked without looking at him.

"Tomorrow," he said. "I get fixed up beginning at nine-thirty and we leave tomorrow evening from Andrews."

"Fixed up?"

"You didn't think I'd just walk into China like this, did you? Ever see a blond Chinese with a Roman nose?"

"A disguise? What will they do?"

"Oh, they've got all kinds of neat tricks now. They'll dye my hair, straighten it, fix my face and hands a bit. I'll be known as Shuang Daw-tse, a humble peasant from the tiny village of Antungwei."

"Where's that?"

"About a hundred miles or so from Tsingtao, the resort where Chang's cover is still laid."

"This isn't *permanent*, is it?"

"Going in, or the disguise?" He grinned at her.

She mock-frowned at him, lowering her eyebrows.

"No," he said seriously. "They've developed a lot of new techniques since Chang's change. His was actually a chemical-medical change, a physiological thing. This'll be mechanical and very temporary. Want to see me?"

"I'm not sure."

"Hang around the apartment until late afternoon. I'll be stopping by to get some things."

She reached for his arm and hugged it, unashamedly, and put her head on his shoulder. "What if something happens?"

"If I get knocked off?" He felt her shudder. "Look, Bernie, this is something we have to do. We'll be all right. This is the last card, and we just have to play it."

"I just don't want you to get caught," she said in a low murmur. She looked up at him and there were tears in her eyes, dew-like droplets that traced a silver-lace network down her cheeks. Her eyes floated in the moist film, and in them he saw her fear, her helplessness.

"Not very subtle, am I?" she said, discouraged. "Bernadette Anne Talbott, Ph.D., paragon of diplomacy, quintessence of intrigue."

"Listen," he said, squeezing her to his chest, cradling her head in his hand, "I know a gal who's shaken old Moser up pretty badly lately, and he's all for it. When I get back I'm heading straight out to her place to stammer out a lot of mushy things. So please don't make it tough now, Bernie, huh?" Moser couldn't finish, instead turning quickly and kissing her hard, his hands cupping her head, pressing her lips to his.

CHAPTER NINE

The tall maples along the parkway marbled the stately front of the Bethesda Naval Medical Center with early morning shadows that waved in a silent pattern across its window-pocked expanse. Moser stepped from the car, and then stopped, fighting a tiny scratch of reluctance. His hands were stiff at his sides, his thumbs nervously flicking along his fingernails. He looked at his watch. Nine-thirty. "Well, at least we're punctual," he said to one of his escorts.

The uniformed man grinned back at him, but said nothing. The other shut the door of the car, and motioned Moser to follow him.

The Naval Medical Center was on the outskirts of Bethesda, Maryland, only a few miles from the Washington city limits. Its multi-functioned complex, embracing several disciplines of experimental and developmental medical research, sprawled near the fairways of the Columbia Country Club, cratered with bean-shaped beige sand traps. They were a pair of country clubs, in fact, if you were to believe the jealous barbs from other service medical personnel about the easy life of the high-ranking physicians there.

But Moser's lot was not going to be easy. He would have to endure several hours of gentle torture under the talented hands of Dr. Bertram W. Freeman, chief surgeon and cosmetician of the Navy's covert Physical Transformation Section. Moser remembered the men he had known at Little Shanghai, men whose transformations were so complete and detailed that it never failed to astonish him, men who spent not hours, but days, of pain and discomfort in sterile laboratories, men he knew he would never see again.

Now Moser was to try for the same effect in less than a single day. He wondered, nervously, if it would be enough, whether the doctor's skill was up to such a complete change in so little time. The skill and efficiency of Dr. Freeman would be the precarious thread on which his life would hang through the days to come.

Moser was led to the second floor of the north research wing. Commander Bertram Freeman, bald and jocular in his crisp white tunic, met him at the end of a brightly lit hallway. "In here, if you please, Captain," he motioned with a smile. "This will be our little beauty shop for this project, for the most part anyway."

Moser tossed his hat on a chair and ran his fingers through his hair. The room was circular, lined in white tile that efficiently reflected the white ceiling light evenly over everything without shadows. "Looks like it was built for surgery," he said.

"Actually, it was. We still do some permanent alterations, special stuff. We've created some pretty bizarre characters lately," he laughed.

"Well, let's hope this one is pretty ordinary," Moser said. "A Chinese that no Chinese would look at twice, next best thing to being invisible."

Dr. Freeman stood by a tall cabinet, studying a sheaf of papers. Across the room, a stainless steel gurney stood covered by a neatly draped white sheet. Over it hovered a menacing, carbon-arc lamp suspended from steel tracks. Around the walls, colorful jars of powders and liquids sparkled against the white tile. It reminded Moser a little of an old-fashioned pharmacy. Or even a barbershop, he thought, as he looked at a padded, multi-position chair with porcelain-handled levers protruding from it like hatpins. Next to it, a cabinet displayed a carefully arranged collection of gleaming chrome and stainless steel instruments, resting like polished silverware on white linen.

Two men in green smocks entered through the swinging doors and began washing their hands and arms in a meticulous rote of procedure, while complaining quietly about the latest rout of the Senators at the hands of the Boston Red Sox. Freeman put down his papers. "Captain," he said, motioning toward the sink, "these are my two assistants, Ensign Jacot and Chief Petty Officer Orr." The two men turned and nodded in order to Moser, then returned to the next step in their prescribed ablutions, brushing their fingernails with a pale green solution. Freeman walked to another cabinet and withdrew a folded white hospital gown. "Well, we might as well get to it, Captain. Follow me, sir."

Freeman led the way to the dressing room as Moser gave a last glance at the carbon-arc monster. "We've made some substantial breakthroughs in recent years, particularly in facial techniques. I'll explain them to you as we proceed. I think you'll find them quite fascinating, if a little uncomfortable."

He opened the door to the dressing room and pointed to another door at the opposite end. "Now, if you'll strip down to the altogether, Ensign Jacot will take you to the anti-bacteria shower. First things first. Have to be clean, you know."

With that, he closed the door and left. As Moser slipped off his tie and began to unbutton his shirt, he thought of how Bernadette would react the next time she saw him. He grinned to himself. She might think it's a monumental practical joke. He hoped Chang would have a chance to prepare her; most of all, he hoped she wouldn't be too worried.

While Moser undressed, Ensign Jacot instructed him on scrubbing himself thoroughly in the high-intensity shower room with a special Phisohex solution and then rinsing with a hot spray of distilled water. Then he was to turn on the cold spray, to close his pores from the ambient bacteria until they were back in the operating room.

Moser listened carefully and began the procedure. Rotating nozzles stung him with thin jets of hot water as he reflexively tried to keep his eyes from the abrasive spray. He lathered and scrubbed his body with a stiff nylon brush. Then he was drenched in an ice-cold solution that smelled vaguely of rubbing alcohol. When the water was turned off, a series of infrared lamps above him came on suddenly, sending amber rays of heat throughout the stall, drying him in seconds. He put on the gown, and followed Jacot back to the operating room.

"You're probably cleaner now than you've ever been in your life," Freeman greeted him. "That anti-bacteria procedure was to prevent retardation of the skin pigmentation by bacterial action on the epidermis. Now then," he said, as he turned to the other technicians, "hand me those facial alteration sketches." He took them and walked over to Moser.

"Want to see what you'll look like?"

He handed Moser a stiff cardboard, on which were pasted a full-front and a side-view photograph of Moser. Attached to the top of the board was a series of overlays, on which were ink sketches. Moser began to place the overlays over the photos, and it was as if he were seeing his face remolded step-by-step, each acetate overlay concealing a feature or adding another. The last overlay showed him the face of an Oriental peasant, and although he saw a slight resemblance to himself, he was surprised at the unexpected result.

Around the periphery of the full-face shot on the last overlay were various code labels, with medical callouts pointing to several areas of the head and contours of the face.

"Doesn't look like I'll ever make it in the Chinese movies," Moser said as he handed the picture back to Freeman. Freeman laughed, then got down to business.

"This is our battle plan, as it were. When we get to treating you facially, these overlays and charts indicate those areas which we'll alter and augment. It should be most effective, judging by your bone structure."

"There'll be no surgery, is that correct?" Moser asked.

"No, it's not necessary any more. Besides, we haven't got the time, even if it were." Freeman squinted at Moser's face, placed his fingers gently on his cheek, and pressed it firmly. "What we now do is alter some of the facial configurations with inserts and rings. Major work will be on the epicanthic folds of the eyes to give you a Mongolian appearance."

Freeman lifted Moser's eyelid with his thumb. "Yours

shouldn't be extraordinarily difficult, though. Do you know that many other races actually possess this fold in their pre-natal life? Disappears, of course, but skin enough remains. Interesting problem for the evolutionists, eh?"

Moser sat back and looked at Freeman. "And the color of the iris—contacts?"

"Yes. They give the illusion of deep brown. A little concern about your cheeks," Freeman pointed to the illustration. "Some work to be done around the buccinator muscles, probably an oral insert. Might be a bit uncomfortable also, but shouldn't obstruct your speech. Ring inserts will be placed in your nostrils. They'll be uncomfortable also, but you'll get used to it. They'll flatten your nose and flare the nostrils. Characteristics of the race."

Freeman spoke with a mixture of professionalism and boyish glee. He obviously enjoyed his work, but it made Moser feel remotely like some sort of specimen, a piece of plastic or silicon, a prone body being beautified by an enthusiastic mortician.

He saw Freeman motion to Jacot, and he and Orr rolled the gurney to the center of the room. Freeman went to a shelf and removed a tiny container of pills that looked like blue-green pearls. "Do you like parsley, Captain?"

"Sometimes. Why do you ask?"

"These capsules contain *methoxsalen*, a derivative of a plant of the parsley family. It's what we call a pigmentation enhancer. It's a rather strong drug used to darken the epidermis, giving it an oily, yellowish pallor, similar to the skin color of central China natives. Actually, we'll use that ultraviolet lamp to begin the darkening process." Freeman pointed to the carbon-arc lamp. "By the end of the day you should be 90 per cent pigmented. Now, if you'll take two of these with this, Captain." Freeman handed Moser two of the pills in a paper cup. Jacot brought him a glass of milk.

"Sounds like instant suntan," Moser said after he swallowed the pills and drained the glass of milk.

"Pretty close," Freeman said. "Actually, it's not very

much different from those artificial suntan lotions on the market. The pills will give you a slight nausea, and perhaps some gastric discomfort, but it will pass, as we say in gastroenteritis circles. The milk will help, too. Now if you'll remove your gown and stretch out on the gurney, we'll start with a massage. A lotion of *dihydroxyacetone*, which is the catalytic element in the indoor suntan lotions, is applied to the epidermis, starting the pigmentation process sooner."

Moser got up and removed his gown. He lay face down on the gurney. Ensign Jacob rubbed the cold greasy liquid on him, front and back, foot and scalp, for nearly twenty minutes. When Jacot was finished, Moser remained on the gurney and waited for Freeman to return to the room. He looked up at the luminous ceiling, relaxing, his thoughts painting pictures of the days to come on the white surface. Freeman's voice interrupted him.

"Well, Captain, how was it?" Freeman was chuckling. "Feel like falling asleep?"

Moser turned his head. "I'll tell you one thing, Ensign Jacot would make someone a wonderful wife."

Freeman smiled and went to the cabinet again. He picked up a mortar and pestle. "You'll get two more of those before the day's out," he called over his shoulder. "Three applications. The effects won't be seen for about four hours, and then you'll notice that the horny parts of your skin, the elbows, balls of your feet, knuckles and so forth, will appear quite dark at first. This will remedy itself as the *methoxsalen* takes over your normal pigmentation processes. The entire effect, by the way, will last for about a week, at which time you'll begin to lighten. It should be long enough, shouldn't it?"

"If all goes well."

"Well, let's hope it does. Wouldn't want to go to all this trouble for nothing. While the *dihydroxyacetone* is drying, we might as well give you a shave. Fortunately, your beard is light, Captain; you shouldn't have to worry about staying closely shaved. Sit in the chair, will you?"

In the chair, Moser's eyebrows were thickened and reshaped, and he jerked and winced slightly as the hairs were plucked. An image of Bernadette flashed past him. She was in a beauty parlor this morning.

The chair was tilted back to a reclining position, and Orr shaved Moser closely and slowly with a specially designed chromium razor. A penetrating depilatory lotion was then applied to his face, and as it stung momentarily, Freeman explained to him how it would retard the growth of facial hair for a few days. "Another curious fact, Captain, is that facial hair grows much faster than scalp hair. Your beard probably grows about a fortieth of an inch a day if it is near average, but you shouldn't have any significant shadow for three or four days."

Freeman took a circular magnifying glass and held it close to Moser's face, peering at him. Moser could feel his breath as Freeman edged along the line of his chin, scrutinizing his throat and sideburns. "Yes. Very good." Freeman was talking mostly to himself, Moser thought, and in an almost diabolical tone, too. "Very good, indeed."

Orr began brushing Moser's hair straight back. Freeman came to the side of the chair. "I said you were quite fortunate in having a light beard, Captain," Freeman said directly. "But I've got some bad news for you, too." He grinned slightly, somewhat embarrassed. Moser looked at him with a quizzical expression.

"Chinese peasants, as I'm sure you know, aren't circumcised."

Moser suppressed a groan.

"This, of course, makes it necessary to attach a latex prepuce."

Moser groaned aloud this time. Freeman ignored him. "It won't cause you much trouble, just a preputial fold in case you're given any cursory physical over there. Anything more careful—well . . ."

Moser nodded slowly. Orr finished brushing Moser's hair, and applied a hair straightener, brushing it in with straight strokes backward. While the straightener processed, Moser's body hair was dyed with a light downy powderpuff. Then his head was washed and dried quickly, and a blue-black dye applied to his hair and eyebrows.

An hour later his hair had undergone a second washing to remove the dye, and he lay on the gurney as two more applications of *dihydroxyacetone* were rubbed into his skin. In between the applications, Moser's smallpox vaccination scar was enlarged slightly, to show that he had been one of the children vaccinated during the great smallpox scare in China years ago, when the missionaries had brought great quantities of vaccine into the nation.

Moser was then made to brush his teeth thoroughly, and Freeman directed Orr to stain them brown with tannic acid. "Too much tobacco and tea," Freeman explained.

"By the way," he went on, "be sure to keep your scalp dirty, Captain. The chance is remote, but your lighter roots could begin to show in a few days. If you notice it, a piece of carbon paper rubbed gently into the scalp will give you a bit more time."

Freeman consulted his papers again, checking Moser over, and then reached for the acetate overlays. "Well, here we go. This will be the most uncomfortable part, the alteration of the epicanthic folds. The cement will sting a bit and cause you to feel like your eyelids are being stretched. Then we'll go with the inserts and rings. Now if you'll take this sedative and lean back and close your eyes."

Before he shut his eyes, Moser looked down at his hands. They were beginning to darken, and he observed the peculiar yellow-brown hue on his knuckles and palms. Then he closed his eyes and watched the darkness change to crimson as a brilliant light hit him in the face.

Again an hour passed. Finally, Freeman stood back, and Moser saw the blackness again. He opened his eyes. Freeman was looking at him, smiling. His stomach began to churn. The pills?

Freeman continued to stare at him. Finally he said, "Captain, I'd like to take some Polaroids of you for our records. This has worked out quite well."

Moser hesitated, then asked, "May I have a mirror?"

Freeman nodded, and Jacot gave him an oval mirror. The hand that reached to accept it wasn't the hand of Jim

Moser. He brought the mirror quickly to his face and looked into it. He saw the staring, shocked face of Shuang Daw-tse.

*   *   *

The golf cart seemed incongruous, a bright red toy, winding its way through the monotonous tan hallways of the underground bowels of the Pentagon. In it, flanked by two Secret Servicemen, President John Robert Burgess and CIA Director Stephenson spoke quietly. The call from an irate and impatient General Galanaugh an hour before had irritated Burgess, but he'd reluctantly consented to come to the LOOK Room to hear Galanaugh out, to let him explain his own plan in full, so that he'd be off Burgess's back for good. The quick-tempered general had sat tight-lipped and disbelieving during the briefing hours ago, and was further enraged when he was directed to order a change in position of the nuclear submarine U.S.S. "Westridge" from its listening post near the coast of North Korea to the peaceful waters near Seoul, Korea. Now he was insisting that Burgess hear him out —hear his own plan to destroy a Cuban submarine out of Havana, which Galanaugh contended was carrying the Red Chinese agent who had forced the confession from Bernadette Talbott. It was, as always, what Burgess had come to refer to in various speeches as "the violence alternative." Now Burgess was about to listen to Galanaugh's particulars, and he had to admit to himself that taking out the sub was, in fact, the only *sure* way to prevent the information from reaching Peking.

"The man's mad," Burgess was telling Stephenson. "He wants to bomb everything. Everything he can't save, he wants to destroy. He just doesn't realize that the repercussions of blowing that sub up could get us in so much deeper we'd never get out."

"Can't *you* do anything about it?" Stephenson asked. "You're Commander-in-Chief, after all."

"A very nice title," Burgess said sarcastically. "But let's face it, Tony, these guys have been running the country too long for me to slap one down without a hearing. No, I'll listen to what he has to say and then just over-rule him. It's the quietest way, I think."

Burgess tugged at his grey sideburn, and reminded himself to get a haircut tomorrow. He looked curiously at the passing doorways and groups of personnel who snapped to attention as the cart passed them. A mental smile of self-consciousness ran through his mind with each smart salute and respectful gaze.

"You know," he said to Stephenson, as the cart turned and started down a long spiral concrete ramp, "I have to admit this beats hell out of Pittsburgh streetcars."

Stephenson grinned. "They say even two-termers never quite get used to being the Chief Executive."

"Still," Burgess said, "sometimes I'm not too sure it isn't better to take orders than to give them."

The cart leveled out and picked up speed as it entered a long, subterranean tube. Blue-white mercury vapor lamps flashed by on either side of them, like a lumines-cent shower of passing meteors. Stephenson puffed on his pipe.

At the end of the tube, the cart came to an abrupt stop. Three guards clicked to attention. Behind them, on a thick glass partition, letters in gold leaf told them where they were:

LOOK ROOM
AUTHORIZED PERSONNEL ONLY

*   *   *

INSERT CODE CARD AND
WAIT FOR I.D. SCAN

Stephenson waved to one of the guards and the other two immediately approached the cart to collect the four code cards. Stephenson was surprised as the guard asked for them.

"This is the President," he said to the guard.

"I'm sorry, sir," the young man said expressionlessly. "I must confirm all identifications."

Burgess, too, was surprised, but said nothing.

"This is ridiculous," Stephenson was saying. "He doesn't *have* a code card. He's the *President.*"

"I'm sorry, sir," the guard repeated. "I have orders."

Burgess leaned forward. "Young man," he said pleasantly, "would you check inside with General Galanaugh? He's expecting me."

The guard saluted and went inside. The other two stood at attention near the door.

"Damn fine job," Burgess said to a distraught Stephenson. "That kid is doing his job and nothing's going to keep him from it. I'm impressed."

They were immediately cleared and ushered inside to a small circular elevator with plain steel walls and no floor indicator. The guard pressed a white button, and the elevator shook momentarily, then began to drop. No one spoke; Burgess began to grow uneasy.

The elevator braked after a long descent, and opened on a climate several degrees cooler than the air-conditioned rooms above. They followed a guard down a corridor which was part hall, part tunnel where the rough-hewn granite had been left bare. Then there was a heavy set of steel doors that gleamed in elegant inconsistency with the stone walls. Burgess watched as the guard slipped a green plastic card into a slot, then snapped back to attention as the door swung ponderously open. They stepped inside as the outer door swung closed again. An automatic blower showered them with a stream of cool, but noticeably drier air, and then another set of doors swung open on the main operations room.

The interior reminded Burgess of a similar room deep within Cheyenne Mountain in Colorado, headquarters for the North American Air Defense Command's total surveillance and strike mission. Burgess had visited it years before when he was a member of the Senate Armed Services Committee.

The first room contained a long bank of Honeywell computers with a dozen technicians and programmers moving among them in puttering attendance. They looked up as Burgess passed, carefully stepping over cables and shielded harnesses, tertiary leads that ran like rubber rivers over the tiled floor.

In the next room a hundred cathode tubes displayed a thousand symbols, figures, maps, binary-coded messages, and pre-programmed messages that flickered quietly across the screens, and splashed reflections along the rows of metal desktops. At each console, a uniformed airman noted every change of data, watched every scan line illuminated on the high-resolution picture tube. Their faces glowed with the grey-green and orange pallor of the phosphors.

Burgess now entered the LOOK ROOM. It was far more elaborate than he'd imagined, with the entire darkened room nearly pulsing in blue and yellow hues from the screens. It was an altar to science, where reverent incantations were whispered in the language of mathematics —a sumptuous cathedral consecrated to technological warfare.

Before the group was a large circular area in which officers in different military uniforms punched buttons, flipped switches, and huddled in hushed conversation. Burgess noted that in this room not one man turned to pay him the slightest attention. To his left, three men sat in leather chairs, but each was sitting forward, hunched over an electronic panel. A second tier held more of the same. So did a third.

A wide-screen, wall-sized display flashed a map of the western hemisphere, and smaller screens arranged around it showed the tactical and offensive strength of every United States and Canadian military base in the world. Unidentified planes and surface vessels were tracked on another set of screens, and still another set showed in coded turquoise symbols the exact strength and armament of each foreign craft. At varied intervals, the display on the large screen would flip instantaneously to another subject: the number and position of airborne craft in the Pacific; strength and status of Minuteman and Polaris deployments; manpower availability at any air base in the world; the course, flight number, origin, and destination of any commercial or private aircraft; the same information for a Russian aircraft straying too close to Greenland's air base. And throughout, the high priests in this ghostly electronic ritual shuffled, whispered, and jotted notes in sacrosanct efficiency—the godlike custodians of the free world's defense and tactical behavior.

Within seconds, General Charles F. Galanaugh strode heavily up to them and snuffed out his cigar in a round aluminum ashtray. "Hello, Charlie," Burgess said softly, glancing about. "What is it you want me to take a look at?"

Galanaugh shook Burgess's hand and nodded to Stephenson. "We're certain the sub is headed for China." Galanaugh led them to a multi-buttoned console. "And pretty soon it'll be too late to head it off." He motioned to an aide.

The large screen flipped to a panoramic projection of the sea area off Maracaibo. Red numerals on the bottom read:

POSIT: 14° 20' 00" NORTH
       68° 14' 21" WEST

An orange pip flashed at one-second intervals within an outlined area on the surface of the water. An adjacent screen showed an enormous real-time sonar display taken by a high-level reconnaissance SR-71, the successor to the U-2.

"That's the sub carrying the agent," Galanaugh said. "We think it'll hug the coast of South America until it gets to Fortaleza, on the Brazilian coast, and then head directly across the Atlantic. Sergeant."

A young man near the console swiped his hand across the face of a panel and the display changed to the coast of China. Burgess saw a red circle around several cities along the foreign coastline. "These are the most likely places of reentry," Galanaugh said urgently. "Haiphong Harbor in North Vietnam, which would be a fast way to get right across the border and into China. We've given that an 'orange' status because of the heavy military traffic in the Gulf of Tonkin. They may decide it's too risky."

Burgess looked at Stephenson and then back at Galanaugh. The general was gesticulating with his unlit cigar, obviously enjoying his performance. Burgess decided to let him finish.

"Next," Galanaugh went on, "we're considering Macao and Hong Kong in the South China Sea. If they know *we* know, they may try a devious way of reentering without our getting to them. But we've given that an 'orange' too, because of the British activity in the area." Galanaugh pointed to another point on the map. "Then, we've got the port of Amoy opposite Taiwan," he said, "but it's also 'orange' because of Nationalist Chinese sea patrols. Now, these six 'red' status points are the most probable entry areas. These are the seaports of Chinhai, Shanghai, Linyunkang, Tsingtao, and most important, Tientsin. Let's have a blowup of those, Sergeant."

The screen changed again and a detailed map of Tientsin zoomed at Burgess. Galanaugh turned to him. "Mr. President, this is important, and the hottest area, because of its proximity to Peking, and because it's closely guarded by the Gulf of Chihli. We've been watching for any signs of new activity, a 'reception committee,' but so far there has been no indication."

"Look, Charlie," Burgess finally said. "How do you know the agent is on that sub?"

Galanaugh shot a puzzled look at Burgess, as if shocked that the reliability of his intelligence sources was being questioned. "One of our agents in Havana reported his boarding, sir. He's *got* to be on it."

"But you're not *sure,* are you?" Burgess insisted.

"We are almost 100 per cent sure, sir. And if he gets to China with the details of the Agreement, we're ruined. Surely you must see how urgent this—"

"I know how urgent it *seems,* Charlie," Burgess said. "But even if the man is still aboard, the documents might be in Cuba! We can't go around blasting foreign subs out of the water because we *think* someone's aboard. Talk about *ruin.* What do we tell everybody, it was an accident?"

"Mr. President," Galanaugh said. "You're sending two

men into the interior to talk an old man into coming out. If they fail, it will be too late and Red China will have the information and beat us to death with it."

"I'd rather risk the lives of two men, Charlie, as callous as that sounds, than run the risk of touching off a war."

"They can't possibly make it, sir," Galanaugh said, nearly pleading with the President. "That sub is the only thing between us and diplomatic disaster."

Burgess turned to Stephenson, then back to Galanaugh. "I'm not sure you understand this completely, Charlie. They are not going in simply to get Tsien. They're going in to keep the Red Chinese from constructing and doing any further development in this new technological area. If they do that, the Talbott Agreement won't matter; it will virtually cease to exist. Now, I know there are many areas in which we disagree, and I'm afraid this is one of them. I can't let you 'remove' a Cuban submarine on the high seas. Continue your surveillance and keep me apprised of the situation."

Galanaugh slumped his shoulders. "We're making a mistake. What about the Russians?"

"If there are mistakes to be made, let me make them, Charlie. I'm sorry, it *has* to be this way. As for the Russians . . . to use the language of the Pittsburgh streets, Charlie, I'll be the first President in much too long a time to tell them to go get fucked!"

Galanaugh's mouth dropped open. Burgess turned and started for the door. Galanaugh walked in the opposite direction, as the screen once again flipped to its Pacific picture.

* * *

At five-thirty that evening the temperature in Moser's apartment was near eighty degrees. Bernadette was cracking a fresh crab for a salad, and Chang Kwok-wah was searching in the refrigerator. He took two bottles of cold beer, and asked Bernadette for an opener. Slowly, she wiped her hands on a towel and searched through the kitchen drawers—finding most of them empty or a jumble of miscellaneous utensils. She moved slowly and carefully, conscious of the lingering soreness on her thighs. She wore a turquoise jersey shift, loosely belted, which was sleeveless and cool. Chang pulled a stool to the counter and poured the beer into glasses, watching the foam surge to the rim. He waved his hand across his face in a fanning motion. "Hot," he said. "Too bad Jim doesn't have an air conditioner."

Bernadette returned to fixing dinner. "I doubt if he could afford one after buying his Porsche." She looked at the clock. "What time do you think he'll be finished?"

"Soon," he said. "We're due at Andrews at eight."

"I wish you didn't have to leave so soon."

"Or that we had left already. I imagine you're anxious to get this whole thing over with." Chang took a sip from the beer and looked at Bernadette. There was no reaction.

"I don't think I'll ever get used to American beer again," he said, turning the conversation to another direction. "I've gotten used to good dark German brew."

"In China? Since when do you get German beer in China?"

"Oh, there once was a brewery in Tsingtao run by the Germans for a long time. No longer, of course. But it is still operating according to the old formulas. Most of it goes directly to the officials."

She finished the salad and put it in the refrigerator to chill, then took her beer and sat down. "I guess it's no secret that I'm in love with Jim."

"None at all. You should have seen his expression when we heard about Boca Raton. He was ready to tear the plane apart."

"He really doesn't *have* to go, does he?"

"He's sure we'll have a better chance of succeeding if the two of us go in." Chang avoided a more direct answer.

Bernadette pulled at her fingers nervously. "Chang, what *would* happen if you got caught? Could you ever get out?"

"No. Eventually we'd be done away with. They'd expose us, make films, extract confessions, all the old tricks to get whatever propaganda they could. Then they'd quietly dispose of us. I'm doing a great job of telling you not to worry."

He was about to go on, to say something—anything—that would set her at ease about the mission's success, but the sound of keys in the lock stopped him. Bernadette gripped the edge of the counter.

Chang stood up. They heard the door open and they walked into the living room. There, beaming proudly, was Shuang Daw-tse. He held out his arms, indicating his new appearance. "Well," he said. "Anybody need a house-boy?"

Bernadette stared. "My God," she exclaimed. "It's astonishing! I don't believe it."

"Excellent," Chang said. "It's an excellent job."

"You're damn right it is," Shuang said. "Those guys over at Bethesda are thorough."

Shuang went over to Bernadette and put his hands on her shoulders. "I know I won't win any 'Smile of the Year' contests, but you're about to get kissed by a very ugly Chinese." He pulled her toward him, and won out over her reluctance, but he kissed her shyly, not quite sure of his new identity.

Chang watched them compassionately. "We don't have much time left," he said gently. "Why don't we have another beer and eat right away, so you two can have some time alone before we leave."

Shuang looked over at him and smiled. Then, in Chinese, he asked, "How's she taking it? Is she okay?"

Chang replied in Chinese, as Bernadette looked from one to the other blankly. "Pretty good. But you'd better do some soothing before you leave. She's worried."

"Okay, you two," Bernadette said. "What are you saying about me?"

Shuang looked at her. "I was just asking him if you'd been a good girl," he said, hugging her.

Chang poured more beer, and they sat at the little kitchen table. Bernadette raised her glass toward them.

Tears filled her eyes. She got up and ran into the bedroom.

Chang Kwok-wah finished his meal alone.

CHAPTER TEN

The Boeing 707-320B, fitted out with a set of finely appointed staterooms normally used by political dignitaries, the press, and high-ranking officials, arched skyward from Andrews Air Force Base the following morning and headed west. There would be a fueling stop at Travis Air Force Base in northern California, and then the polished silver jet, with its crew of seven and its two precious passengers, would race the sun across the shimmering waters to the Orient.

Chang Kwok-wah and Shuang Daw-tse spent most of their time in the forward cabin, rehearsing the details of their entry. The teacher-student role was reversed now, as Chang made Shuang Daw-tse repeat his background, his personal history, his family. Chang drilled him incessantly on his life as a peasant, the foods he ate and the new modes of behavior since the Communist upheaval of social customs. Shuang had studied the new written language, too, even though he was supposed to be an illiterate. The simplified Chinese characters, according to Mao Tse-tung, would bring about a rise in the read-and-write education of China. In reality, it was only another rancid leaf in the bitter tea of China.

Chang stared at Shuang, examining his face, scrutinizing every line and wrinkle as if for the first time. Shuang spoke endlessly into a portable Ampex, as Chang studied and criticized his speech patterns, listening for irregularities in inflection and meaning. Over and over Shuang repeated the endless phrases.

They were both dressed in light-blue jump suits for the flight; their clothes, identification papers, coupons, were stowed aboard the U.S.S. "Westridge," awaiting their arrival.

They spoke Chinese exclusively now, their voices chanting a musical litany in three octaves. "But Davis," Chang spoke evenly, "if he's there, won't be able to hang around very long."

"You're to make the contact?"

"It'll be better if you stay in the background as much as possible. Stay close behind me, but don't say anything. I'll risk the contact because Davis wouldn't have any reason to be talking to a peasant. I'll just get the location of the escape boat, and walk directly to the University. There should be a message for us on the 'Westridge' as to how we'll recognize him."

Shuang twisted his face into a frown. "I can just vaguely remember who he was. One of the first ones?"

"He was right behind me in the pilot class. In fact, he was in the adjacent cell the time they pulled that loyalty test on us. I never knew him well, though."

"What happens if we miss him?"

"Nothing."

"Nothing?"

"We'll have to get out the best way we can. If there's no boat waiting for us, we'll just have to get one. I don't know."

Shuang knew the pitfalls well and didn't know why he had asked the question. The palms of his hands were moist, and he wiped them on the knees of his jump suit.

"The main thing," Chang continued, "is to say as little as possible. Act bewildered. Befuddled. Use hand motions whenever you can instead of speaking. Act like you're enjoying all the official attention."

Shuang took out a map of the University of Peking, and the two men pored over it.

Chang pointed at one area. "Now here's where they train the students. Tsien's office is here. His house is located . . ."

*   *   *

The plane slowly lost its race with the sun, and as darkness began to engulf them, they ate a steak dinner. Then the dwindling arc of crimson sun slid over the western horizon, and they slept.

Nine hours later they began to lose altitude. Below them Seoul lay wrapped in a cocoon of fog. A misty patchwork of fires and lights glimmered in an orange grill. They began their descent. The runway was blurred, partially obliterated in the grey-black evening, and Shuang watched the damp ground slip by as the heavy plane began to drop.

Chang had been asleep since midnight. Shuang glanced at his wrist, wondering about the time, and caught himself. A mistake. Got to be careful. An involuntary action like turning your wrist to your face would instantly tear away the disguise of a poverty-stricken peasant. He looked at the bulkhead over the cabin door: "0200 hours."

Seoul. The name of the city rang with memories for Shuang. Years ago he had been here with the 7th Fleet, after his tour of duty on Formosa. He remembered a prostitute he once knew. Where was she now? An old man who once gave him directions. Him? Dead now, probably, both of them. Either killed in the Korean War, or by disease or starvation. And he thought of how anxious he'd been to return to the States, to American women with blonde hair and lily-smooth skin, and even white teeth. Women who were perfumed with vanilla-sweet scents, instead of the stench of fish and poverty.

It hadn't happened that way, though. Immediate assignment to Little Shanghai. No blondes. Now he was on his way to the Orient again, into the starving villages and filthy throngs of panic-faced peasants. And he was to be one of them.

The Boeing banked sharply to starboard as it adjusted its landing path and lumbered lower. Shuang heard the familiar *thunk-thunk* of the wheels being lowered and locked. Chang stirred momentarily and his head jerked forward as the plane hit the runway. Shuang flicked his fingernails nervously as he watched the stroboscopic lights on the runway's edge urging the plane onward, throwing slower and slower patterns of white light across Chang's cheek. Chang stirred anew, and Shuang reached over and shook him awake.

* * *

The special briefing room at Osan Air Force Base in Seoul was stark and ringed with the pale grey of blackboards. A map of the Orient hung on one wall, with long-forgotten red pins stuck randomly into it. There was a small steel desk, and nine steel chairs. A coffee pot gurgled on a rusty hotplate. A sepia picture of the base commandant looked down on them.

A young master sergeant gave them a manila envelope, and said, "Commander Hodges will be with you in a moment, gentlemen. His helicopter's just arriving. You may want to read this while you're waiting." The young man's features were weasel-like, his face pointed. Shuang, for some reason, didn't like him. Perhaps it was his official tone, his austere manner. Perhaps Shuang's anxiety was making him irritable. He reminded himself mentally once again to remain careful, to be patient and stoic. Just as the automatic glancing at his nonexistent watch could cost him his life, so could impatience, sudden anger, reflect his non-Oriental temperament. He glanced at Chang and opened the manila envelope.

RED MASK FILE 4635
TO: CAPT. MOSER, JAMES F., 277451 USN
MESSAGE: DAVIS REPORTS CHANG'S COVER
   STILL IN EFFECT—PROCEED AS OUTLINED IN
   ATTACHED   SCHEDULE—CONTACT   DAVIS
   YOUR OWN DISCRETION—IF POSSIBLE BE
   AVAILABLE EXACTLY 1700 HRS 10 AND 11
   AUG IN COURTYARD SUMMER PALACE NEAR
   BRIDGEWAY ON SOUTH SIDE—CONFIRMED
   —DAVIS WILL HAVE CAMERA ASAHI PEN-
   TAX WITH TRIPOD ON SHOULDER STRAP—

YELLOW BADGE READING "PROSPERITY"—
CONTACT CODE: WHERE IS THE WALKWAY
TO THE AUTUMN PROMENADE?—RESPONSE
CODE: FROWN AT PEASANT WITH CHANG
AND WORDS: IT IS THE FINEST TIME FOR
TAKING PICTURES—HE IS TO HAVE INFO ON
ESCAPE BOAT TIENTSIN—GOOD LUCK——
STEPHENSON

Shuang looked into the envelope again and took out
nine typewritten sheets filled with times, dates and plans,
places and alternative exit areas should something un-
planned develop. One sheet detailed their rendezvous—it
was called "Point Sierra."

As Chang finished reading the message Shuang had
handed him, they were interrupted by the appearance of
Commander Gerald P. Hodges. He was a tall, broad-
shouldered man with a thin, chiseled mouth and thick
eyebrows. His salt-and-pepper hair was long, unruly, with
a cowlick that stuck out in the rear. His chin and nose
were angular; the latter obviously had been broken. His
entire visage reflected unchallenged authority. Hodges
had been in the submarine service since the beginning of
World War II, and it showed. Shuang Daw-tse had heard
his name many times, the man's legendary exploits, and
had liked what he'd heard.

"Tricky little problem here, Moser," Hodges said without shaking hands. Then, "By the way, gents, which one
of you's Moser?" He sat on the edge of the desk and
looked down at the two seated Chinese.

"Here," Shuang Daw-tse said. "It's Shuang. This is
Chang Kwok-wah."

"All right, Shuang," Hodges said. "The trick here is to
get in as close as we can. The goddam Chicom sonar set-
ups are everywhere, but they're pretty inefficient. Stone-
age stuff. We sure as shit can't hang around too long,
though, and it'll be chancey trying to get in too close. The
'Westridge' is pretty well equipped; we've been playing
around in the Korean Bay for the last several months.
But your timing is going to have to be phenomenal if

we're going to pick you up and get you out okay. One mile is the closest I'll risk."

Hodges got up and drew out a map of the area and plastered it on top of the desk, shoving the coffee pot aside. The three men huddled over the desk. But Shuang, in a fleeting vision, saw the day when he no longer had to look at another map in his life.

"They've got patrols all over the goddam place," Hodges said, as he stabbed a hairy index finger onto the map. "Getting in'll be harder than getting out, actually. And you poor freaks will have to contend with coastal guards and probably some sentry dogs after you ditch your raft. We'll have no way of knowing what the hell is going on in there, so I have to stress one point. If you're not at Point Sierra at precisely twenty-two hundred hours, we take off and leave you to the sharks. You're going to get awfully sick of my telling you that before we're through."

"I don't even know the train schedules from Peking," Chang said. "Can't you give us some leeway?"

"*Leeway?*" Hodges grunted. "Christ, we can't just sit there like a wooden mallard and wait for them to bomb the shit out of us. No, it's pick up and leave. Sorry."

Shuang eyed Hodges coldly, still self-conscious about his appearance. "What about an alternate time? An alternate point in case we get hung up? In case we're still in the area."

"Listen, you guys," Hodges said heavily. "I don't know what the hell you're up to in there, or what in God's name you're going to do, because all I do is follow orders. I do know that I'm pretty goddam pissed-off about having to risk ninety-nine damn good men aboard the 'Westridge.' If it were up to me, I'd send you in on a goddam sampan, but these orders came directly from Admiral Landor himself. I'm not about to wait around to get blown the hell out of the water just so you two CIA biggies can save your asses. If you're not at that pickup point within one minute of twenty-two hundred hours, it's just tough tittie."

Chang looked up in surprise at Hodges' bluntness.

Shuang accepted his black-and-white professionalism. He'd been in the Navy himself far too long not to understand the man's concern for the safety of both his men and the submarine. No shades of grey. And the first tiny black teeth of fear began to chew at the walls of his stomach.

"Now then," Hodges went on, looking at Chang, "can you give me anything more on their radar and sonar installations at Chinching?"

Chang shrugged. "Nothing," he said, "except that it's not too well built-up. Tsingtao is a resort, mostly."

"Can't be too sure about anything over there," Hodges said. "Things might work out. We can cruise at about thirty-five knots at about a hundred feet most of the way. Nearer to the surface when we get closer in. To get from Tsingtao to Point Sierra will take about fifteen hours. So we'll wait on the bottom of Chihli until twenty-two hundred."

"Do they mine the harbor at Tsingtao?" Shuang asked Hodges.

"Some," Chang said before Hodges could answer. "But Kiaochow Bay is used mostly for fishing and recreation, so it's doubtful."

"We can detect their mine fields," Hodges said. He folded the map and placed it in a leather case. "Let's get to the 'Westridge.' There's a chopper outside, and your gear's already aboard."

*   *   *

The chopper hovered a few hundred feet over the grey waters until a black form loomed up to the surface and broke the water with a spray of white foam: the U.S.S. "Westridge" rolling and swaying like a black prehistoric dolphin. She had no markings except the number "Thirty-nine" stenciled in white on her conning tower. She was nine years old, a 252-foot attack submarine of the *Skipjack* class, converted into a reconnaissance ship. Unlike others of her class—smooth and lean—her conning tower was a confusing array of antennas, parabolic reflectors, and Cassegrain transmitters. It was a good ship, built in Norfolk, and Hodges was her first commander. The "Westridge" was a far cry from the "pigboat" on which he had learned the submariner's trade. She could cruise at speeds up to thirty-five knots and operated comfortably up to one-thousand-foot depths. For the past eighteen months, the "Westridge" and her crew of ninety-nine specialists had been cruising submerged along the North Korean coast, eavesdropping on internal communication and broadcasts from Radio Pyongyang. Most of the time she kept radio silence and surfaced only at night so that Chinese hydrographic vessels and trawlers couldn't calculate her position. She was rated in "Four o" shape—excellent.

But she's a paid coward, Shuang thought as the chopper's winch lowered him to the heaving deck. She's under orders to run from trouble, to protect the priceless electronic gear that bulged her belly, to avoid the slightest danger of contact. The Yellow Sea teemed with destroyers, subchasers, and even smaller craft that buzzed around British and American ships like gnats—and the government didn't want another "Pueblo."

He made his way across the slimy deck toward a young officer who waited to help him below. Shuang was surprised at the sub's size. He had only seen photographs of *Skipjack* class. They were probably only preliminary drawings in the days when he had withdrawn from the Navy of the sea and joined the strange, land-bound ship called Little Shanghai. Below, she was palatial in comparison to Shuang's memory of the old, non-atomic subs, even though it was apparent that every spare foot had been commandeered to house her special electronic gear: a complete communications center, data processing computers and peripheral hard-and-software, underwater search gear, and noise analysis instruments. Most were obviously built to her unique specifications because they neatly followed the curvature of her hull and molded themselves to make best use of the space.

Hodges and Chang had joined him within minutes and, as the hatches thunked shut, the sub dived silently into the cold protection of the deep sea. They were given a cursory tour of the ship, Hodges leading the way. But although they walked what seemed like more than a mile on several decks, Hodges was careful to skirt certain key data-handling and decoding areas, and pointedly neglected to explain the function of several impressive instruments.

He stopped in one of the navigation compartments, however, to explain the derivation of "Point Sierra," their rendezvous point. It was a movable point, he explained, used by the Navy to deliver and collect agents in the Yellow Sea, Korea Bay, and the Gulf of Chihli. Though it was seldom used, its location was constantly changed according to location of fleet units, and to avoid the constantly changing patterns of harbor traffic as reported directly from SR-71 surveillance. For this mission, "Point Sierra" would be a spot one mile off the Hopei coast opposite Tientsin—precisely 118° 17′ north and 39° 41′ 23″ east.

"Your gear is in here," Hodges said as they reached their cabin. "May as well get yourselves ready. We'll be approaching Tsingtao at twenty-one hundred hours tomorrow. In the meantime, catch up on your sleep. I'll have something sent in for you to eat."

With that, Hodges left the cabin, closing the hatch behind him. Shuang looked through his gear. There was a faded and torn brown shirt of crude cloth, black, pajama-type trousers of rough burlap, and a pair of worn and stained hard wooden sandals. A set of dirty papers identified him as Shuang Daw-tse, a peasant from Antungwei, and head of a family of seven. There was a tattered cheap paperback reprint of Chairman Mao's aphorisms, as well as a booklet of rice-allotment coupons. Ostensibly these could get him a sack of rice with which to feed his family for a month, but it was scarcely enough for a week. Then there was his performance record, a straw sun hat, and a soiled rag stuffed into the shirt's only pocket.

Chang's clothes and papers had been replaced, and were identical to those he had carried with him when he left the conference at Canton University. They undressed and began to put the clothes on.

"Are all you Navy men as direct as Hodges?" Chang asked as he tried the *Jem-ming* on for size.

Shuang couldn't resist a smile. "Doesn't mince words, does he? Most of the sea-going types are like that." He put his sandals on and stood up, testing them. The right one pinched his instep. "Do you think I'll get any grilling before we get to the university?"

"Doubt it. Anyone who stops us will respect my position. I should be able to talk them down easily enough, but at the university it'll be a different matter."

"What about Davis? I can't get over the feeling that whether we get out or not rests squarely with him, alternate exit or no."

"He's a good man," Chang said. "I remember how reliable he was at Little Shanghai. He didn't crack in the prison. Don't worry. If it's up to him, everything will be there when we need it."

They finished dressing in silence. When they were through, satisfied that their clothes were in proper order they inspected each other. It was a sharp contrast. A refined, respected scientist, resplendent in the finest blue wool jacket, tall, handsome, self-assured. Next to him a filthy peasant, stooped and fearful, eyes darting suspiciously, ready to drop to his knees in frightened obedience to anyone's command.

Hodges returned to the cabin. Behind him was a seaman holding a tray with two hot meals on it.

"You boys really got yourselves some backing," he said, grinning for the first time since they'd met him. "This just came over the decoder from Washington." He handed Shuang a yellow sheet of teletype paper, and Chang looked over his shoulder as they read it.

RECONFIRMATION OF SUB ROSA POLLING SHOWS U.N. VOTE FAVORABLE—EVERYTHING RESTING WITH YOU NOW AS TO HOW WE GET OUT OF THIS MESS—GOOD LUCK AND HOPE TO SEE YOU FOR DRINKS IN FOUR DAYS. . . . JOHN ROBERT BURGESS

Chang looked up at Hodges. Hodges said, "You're really on the spot, fellas. I still don't know what it's all about, but you've got a helluva lot of guts, I'll say that for you." Shuang, more than the other Chinese, knew how high the praise was.

Then Hodges and the seaman left, leaving the steaming tray on a table bolted to the floor. Chang noted a cup of tea on the tray. "They went all out for us on this food," he said.

"Navy chow is the best in the armed forces, friend."

*   *   *

They heard a deep-throated gurgling as the salty water from Kiaochow Bay filled the "Westridge's" submersion tanks, and they shoved off, bobbing precariously in the churning, murky water. They peered over the lip of the black rubber raft. The conning tower of the "Westridge," like a giant dorsal fin, cut through foamy moonlit bubbles and disappeared, leaving a plume of white on the surface. The raft pitched in the wake, and they lay prone listening to the receding rumble, saying nothing.

Cautiously, they reached for the oars and began to paddle. A bitter, cold wind whipped at the raft, sending freezing drops of salt spray into their faces. Shuang's fingers were growing numb, but his body stayed warm in his wet suit. He watched Chang and saw the other man slowly working his arms, eyeing the inky blackness ahead of him.

The moon was one-quarter. There were no clouds, and the stars blinked down impersonally from the China sky. The endless stretch of dark water occasionally flashed with needlepoint sparks of reflected moonlight. The water lapped at the raft.

What seemed like hours later, the Tsingtao coast began to loom hard and harsh, the mountains jutting into the sky like mangled fists. The contour of the mountains of this region had always fascinated Shuang. They were twisted hulks, unfinished mounds from the Pleistocene age, that made a sharp, deformed silhouette against the star-dusted sky. A hazy mist was settling on Tsingtao it-

self, far to their right and northward. A fire burned somewhere along the shore, above where they were to beach
the raft. Probably a guard or shoreline patrol camp,
Shuang surmised.

The wind gusted again as the water cradled the raft in
a rhythmic rocking. Shuang watched as Chang took a
compass the size of a silver dollar from a plastic bag and
studied its fluorescent face. He motioned back to
Shuang, pointing to a spot on the shore. They continued
to paddle, more slowly now, more carefully, eyes strained
against the carbon shore, watching for signs of activity.
They were about a thousand yards from the beach.

A rocky arm of land reached toward them to the right,
obscuring their landing area from the harbor of Tsingtao.
Chang motioned to keep paddling straight ahead. Shuang
looked to his rear and watched the fire disappear behind
the jetty. Fifty yards ahead, he could make out the forms
of two light-colored rowboats docked at what looked like
a platform of some sort. Nearby, a breakwater, made of
crumbling hunks of concrete and cement, stuck into the
water. They headed to the left of it. "We're to the southeast of the city," Chang whispered. "Most likely what's
left of a communal farm. The resort's north of here, and
west."

Somewhere a dog barked as they neared the beach. It
was a plea, a helpless yelp, rather than a warning. The
sand came closer, and the raft washed almost ashore.

In seconds they were out of the raft, pulling it up, and
stepping briskly through the wet sand, scurrying toward
the thick, protective brush a hundred feet from the water's edge.

They quickly deflated the raft and peeled off their wet
suits, their carefully fabricated costumes dry underneath.
Shuang tucked the wet suits into one of the folds of the
raft along with the paddles. They buried the bundle in the
loose sand, smoothing it carefully. Chang stood up and
peered into the darkness. The dog whined again.

Then the two men scurried through the protection of
the brush, skirting along the sandy strip toward the sleeping city of Tsingtao.

* * *

Tsingtao sits on the southern edge of the Shantung Peninsula. It is four hundred miles from Peking, a distance lengthened by the meandering course of the railway. The ancient road winds through grotesque mountains eastward from Tsingtao to Tsinan, then north to Tientsin and Peking. Although no official census has been taken since 1936, the Chinese government places the population of Tsingtao at one and a half million. Its wharves, some distance from the resort area, are a disorganized jumble of tin huts, junks, sampans, lean-tos, and cardboard shacks. It is a poor town with homeless and abandoned children walking the streets by day and sleeping under trees or in doorways by night.

Chairman Mao's "Great Leap Forward" had demanded heroic efforts to relieve food shortages by extracting more and more from the land. But so far the indiscriminate use of chemical fertilizers had left much of the land arid and sterile, too barren for even the humblest of grains. Communal farms throughout the rolling grasslands to the west have fields planted in oats and barley, but harvests have been pitifully sparse.

A few miles away from the city, however, lies another world. Beyond the struggling farms, past rice paddies and tapioca trays, past primitive blast furnaces set up for the hasty "back yard" production of pig iron, lies the Resort of the Blue Fawn, where those chosen by the government may occasionally vacation as a special reward for patriotic service or singular accomplishment.

Chang and Shuang reached Tsingtao at dawn as the morning sun was already evaporating the moisture from the streets of the city. Citizens were awakening punctually to a new day of labor, of poverty, and of government-supervised exercise. The older men and women were out first, gathering in parks and litter-strewn squares throughout the city. Then came the younger people, most of them dressed in khaki uniforms, chanting and leaping their way through the prescribed ritual for physical fitness in the People's Republic. As the two Chinese hurried through the narrow streets they paused to watch a group of balding Mandarins practicing the tranquil motions of *T'ai Chi Ch'uan*, a series of 108 positions for unarmed self-defense. Chang led them on their way, skirting the main part of the city, staying close to the wharves. The fishermen had already gone, their women waiting silently, suckling babies or selling fish. In one of the merchant stalls they watched a skinny wisp of a man, toothless, but with the stub of a cigarette alternately clamped between his gums or hanging loose from his lower lip. He was slowly, mechanically, chopping the heads off chickens he pulled from a wire cage. They looked nearly dead already from malnutrition.

Through these streets even walking was difficult. Every space not appropriated by fish-sellers or merchants or trampled by the aimlessly wandering throng was cluttered with children or with groups of old people, idly playing *Mah-jhong* and awaiting death, ignored by a government too caught up in a frenzy of youth development to care about those without a useful future. Shuang was relieved when they reached the road leading out of town.

The arcade leading to the main entrance of the Resort of the Blue Fawn was magnificent. Flower beds and ponds were everywhere, larger lakes with sculptured flower islands, waterfalls that fell into pools flashing with fish and ruled by black and white swans. The gardens and grounds were immaculate, embroidered on a smooth green carpet that stretched in splendor all the way to the shoreline beaches.

Chang had no trouble at the entrance. It was Shuang's first test and as he waited for Chang to make explanations, his demeanor was perfect. When the guard asked his birthplace, he responded humbly, being careful to look with respect at Chang before replying, showing his reluctance to speak in his prestigious presence without direct consent. The guard was impressed and treated Chang with even greater deference.

They walked directly to the resort office inside the courtyard where Chang had been instructed to register. Shuang trotted behind him as they approached. Then, at the door, Chang turned and motioned him to a halt, then stepped up to the official. The guests in the courtyard eyed Shuang scornfully. A peasant at the Resort of the Blue Fawn? A dirty laborer allowed to mingle with China's elite scientists and politicians? But when they followed Shuang's adoring gaze into the office doorway and saw Chang Kwok-wah standing masterfully before the official, they hid their scornful glances and strolled away. Surely, they thought, this was an exalted man, someone who must have only the best of reasons to bring this peasant with him.

Chang spoke in an authoritative but apologetic tone. He was sorry to disgrace the Resort of the Blue Fawn with the presence of this low and uncouth fellow, but his mission was an important one and this poor peasant held important intelligence for Mao's government. That was why it was necessary for Chang to contact his superior in Peking immediately and return to duty instead of enjoying the honor of their hospitality. He would leave the resort as soon as he had notified Dr. Tsien Hsue-shen. He could be in Peking by nightfall, could he not?

The mention of Dr. Tsien brought a raised eyebrow and the official immediately burrowed through his desk for a train schedule. Yes, indeed he could. And the official himself would be most grateful for the honor of making the travel arrangements for him. As he disappeared with a bow into an inner office, Chang stepped to the doorway and called harshly to Shuang, ordering him to remain where he was and say nothing to the distinguished guests or he would be dealt with later. Shuang bowed low in an attempt at elegance and Chang was pleased to see that his awkward hesitation made him seem even more the pitiful peasant.

Chang was offered the use of the official's telephone and called a message to Dr. Tsien's office. Then the official returned with rail reservations and Chang apologized once again for his inability to partake of the famous pleasures of the resort. The official bowed, inviting Chang in respectful tones to return to the Blue Fawn as quickly as he could.

A car was waiting to drive the pair to the nearby train station. As they drove down the lane, a flurry of crimson-feathered birds thrashed upward like tossed confetti from a pond, disappearing as they melted into the red of the morning sun.

As they waited alone on the platform, Shuang exhaled gratefully. "How did I do?" he asked.

"Perfect," Chang replied. "That was the first hurdle. Now they get higher and harder."

Shuang was silent for a minute, breathing deeply now that he dared to eschew his cramped and humble slouch. Then, "What's our first stop?"

"First thing we do in Peking is try to contact Davis. We have to be sure the boat is ready. Then I'll get in touch with Tsien. I've already left a message with his office. You probably won't be invited to his house, you know. Just the university."

The train was only a half-hour late. It was a twenty-year-old engine faltering at the head of a chain of five rickety cars. Amid frowns and stares of scorn directed at Shuang Daw-tse, they boarded and found seats. The train pulled out of the station with a rude jerk and rocked along through the rolling hills of Shantung Province. Near Weifang, they looked out on gangs of working men, girls and boys, mutual-aid teams developing agricultural cooperatives on the striated hillsides. The men were pulling crude iron plows which the girls guided into the hard and barren ground. On gentler slopes wheat was being harvested by men on reapers pulled by thin and sway-backed horses.

They said nothing throughout the long trip. Two Red Guards were seated directly behind them.

* * *

In Peking's Forbidden City, near the Gate of Heavenly Peace, the militiamen were holding a rally as Chang and his peasant companion arrived. As they crossed the large, white-stoned courtyard, a group of fifty new recruits, each wearing bandoliers and carrying long, bayonetted rifles, clapped their hands gleefully. Their blue-clad leader screamed instructions and exhortations, and they replied in unison. The new soldiers, dressed in various shades of blue, sat cross-legged in neat rows. Around them the older guards sat and joined in their clapping, exhorting them to new fervor as they prepared for their first service to the revered Mao, the "education"—or the purging and looting—of a nearby town.

The sun shone down brightly in the midafternoon heat. Elsewhere around the Gate of Heavenly Peace sightseers strolled casually, preparing for the Autumn Promenade into the Inner City, an annual ceremony designed to make the citizens of Peking believe they had gained new freedom under the enlightened Republic. Some of them carried cameras, some led groups of children and they walked smiling among the sculpture and the huge Chinese characters hewn from stone. In the near distance, the bright red and brown roof of the Central Palace loomed majestically. Once it was the residence of emperors but now it belonged to the people—for one day a year.

They were to meet Davis at the far end of a long arcade. Its roof was a mass of intricate carvings, brightly lacquered, and inlaid with ivory. The walls glowed with a hundred lacquer coats and were laced with delicate red and purple floral designs. Sightseers strolled in and out of its archways and clusters of Red Guards walked up and down the area—sullen, angry men and boys who seemed hungry for violence, who seemed to be searching for new ways to use their government-bestowed power.

Shuang followed one step behind the dignified Chang. Now and then he would turn and grunt an order, reminding any observers that he was a peasant following his master, therefore not to be disturbed.

Chang stopped suddenly and reached for his shoe. Then he called to the peasant behind him. Shuang knelt, removed Chang's right shoe and shook out an imaginary stone. "He's there," Chang whispered, "but I don't like it."

A man stood near the archway behind a 35 mm. Pentax mounted on a tripod. Two other men lounged nearby against the archway, looking out into the faces of the

crowd. Shuang peered up from between Chang's legs. It
was Davis, all right. He wore a blue linen *Jem-ming* of
lower quality than Chang's but good enough to mark him
as an official—the leader of a large labor force at work
near Peking who was taking a few days off for sightseeing
during the autumn ritual. The two men didn't seem to be
paying any attention to him. "We'll have to chance it,"
Shuang whispered back. Then he replaced Chang's shoe
and bowed to his master as he rose.

Chang nodded and they turned, looking cautiously
around them. Then, as if he made up his mind to ask for
information or directions, Chang took a half step toward
the photographer. At that instant, Davis snapped his tripod shut and whirled toward the two men behind him.
He shouted at them in *Wu,* the language of the provinces
around Shanghai, adding to the intended confusion, since
the citizens of Peking, heart of Mandarin country, never
deigned to understand "lower dialects."

"Pigs," he shouted at them, "how can I take pictures
when your fat forms hide the light of the sun? Will no
one leave the artist to his work? Away, or I must break
your unworthy bodies against the gates of our holy capital!" As he swung at them, using the folded tripod and
camera as a club, one man lunged at him, catching him
with a lightning blow to the solar plexus. The other man
drew a gun and then a whistle. He blew a single, sharp
blast.

Chang checked his turn in mid-stride and skirted the
melee with a distasteful manner appropriate to his rank.
Almost as they passed, a platoon of soldiers approached
the gate at a dead run. As he turned to grunt an order at
Shuang, Chang noticed that they were sealing off the area
of the arcade. "The traitor is caught, the traitor is
caught," one was squealing in high-pitched Mandarin.
Seconds later a car sped past them, carrying a uniformed
driver and two men in official dress. K'ang Sheng's men,
Chang thought to himself, and kept on walking.

"My God," Shuang breathed when they were alone.
"They've got him. Can't we do anything?"

"Of course not. That's why he did it," Chang answered

evenly, stoically hiding the tragedy he felt gnawing within him. "They must have had him under surveillance when he was trying to arrange for the boat. He knew there was nothing he could do for us but he had to warn us. Otherwise we might have asked someone about him—and the someone probably would have been one of K'ang Sheng's boys." Chang took a long breath, then continued in a softer tone. "He didn't have enough time to lay a cover."

"Suicide." Shuang felt a knot of despair grow in his throat, spread hot and painfully through his craven, Oriental body.

"It was the only way," Chang said.

Shuang looked straight ahead of him as they walked on, occasionally glancing around when something caught his eye, some flash of color on a billboard, a group of soldiers marching in cadence, a particularly impressive building. "The poor son of a bitch," he said at one point, and then walked the rest of the way in silence.

They reached the University of Peking without incident, but at the main gate, after Chang entered the guardhouse to check in, a guard looked long and hard at Shuang. Then, in an instant, a second guard had seized him from behind.

"Who are you?" the first guard snarled. "What are you doing away from your commune?"

Shuang was startled and his frightened eyes looked around for Chang—and caught him as he stepped out of the guardhouse. Chang read the message of panic and, before the guard could speak again, he waved his hand within inches of the second guard's face and shouted in a voice dipped in anger.

"Let him go, you pig! This man is with me. I'm taking him inside on university business!"

The guard let Shuang go and stepped back, startled. "Taking *him* inside?" the first guard asked.

"Yes, you fools. Why don't you check before you begin mauling people? We're going to the office of Dr. Tsien in the morning. I'm to escort this peasant to his residence room until then."

"What *is* the business?" the guard asked officiously. "What *kind* of business?"

"That's no concern of yours," Chang said abruptly, knowing he had gained the upper hand. "Just check his papers and let us through. We cannot stand here all day!"

The guard mumbled, examined their papers and waved them through. He whispered something to the second guard as they passed. He sneered.

"What do we do about the boat?" Shuang asked as they walked alone across the university lawn.

"Nothing," Chang said. "We'll just have to find one when we get to the coast."

"Why not get to Tsien tonight? That would give us more time to find one."

"We can't risk it," Chang said. "His house is full of relatives. We'd never get out. Tomorrow is better."

"That guard didn't sound as if he believed you."

"We have to assume he did. Our papers were in order or he would have raised a fuss to save face."

"What do I do tonight? Won't they ask me questions?"

"I doubt it," Chang said as they drew near the entrance to the multi-storied building. "In the first place, you're my guest and you're sure to have a room alone. Besides, who'd want to bother with you? Have you looked at yourself lately? Or taken a deep breath?" Chang smiled warmly.

"Well, I'll be damn glad when it's over," Shuang said. "It's going to be tough enough getting a boat, much less finding Hodges on time."

They walked up the stairs in silence, too near to be seen in a conversation between equals. Christ, Shuang thought. They got Davis! Nearly five years of this crap, and doing a helluva job, too. The irony of it struck him. *He* had been there when Davis was inducted into RED MASK, nine thousand miles away at Little Shanghai. And now here he was again. The beginning and the end. The first smile, the last tear.

What if it had been him? What if he were caught and questioned? Or seized by the Red Guards or K'ang Sheng's men. Would Chang risk his life or his assignment to help him? No. Of course not. He could be tortured or killed, no matter. Chang would walk calmly away, complete the mission if he could, or resume his identity and look for another way. They were here for one thing—to remove the threat of Tsien and get the word back to Stephenson. They were not important, only the deed.

CHAPTER ELEVEN

Dr. Tsien Hsue-shen's six-block house near the University of Peking was one of the finest in the city. Visitors entered through the swinging gates on *Tsien's Wu-tong*, the street named after the doctor. They stepped into a sculptured formal garden, turned left past the guard house, and crossed the courtyard toward the first level. A school, which was attended by the children of the family, stood to the left, facing a row of small guest houses, which in turn formed an "L" with the main house. Behind the guest houses lay a private garden with cement urns of swimming fish buried flush with the surface. Here the family and their guests could stroll in solitude. Behind the main house, which consisted of a dining room and living room, was another, still larger garden and a repetition of the rows of guest houses facing across a larger courtyard to another main house, this one with three rooms instead of two. This arrangement repeated itself for six blocks, each successive courtyard and main house becoming larger and more formal, each garden more elaborately planted with larger and more impressive shrubbery and flowers. Finally, there was the house in which Dr. Tsien and his family lived, an elegant, eight-room house where the scientist entertained the most important of his many guests. All told, Dr. Tsien employed eighteen full-time gardeners.

Chang Kwok-wah had escorted the peasant Shuang

Daw-tse to his assigned residence room at the university without incident. The room was near the laboratory where Chang and Dr. Tsien had worked on their psychokinesis tests.

He cautioned Shuang again to say nothing, to volunteer no information, and to stay quietly in his room until Chang returned to report on the evening's conference with Dr. Tsien. But, as he neared the entrance to Tsien's home, Chang felt a moment of worry about Shuang. Would someone stop to question him? Might a servant "drop in" to chat and shake the thin fabric of Shuang's cover dossier? He put his fears behind him and, as he strode through the main gates, he set his mind in readiness for the coming feast, hoping that most of the family and guests would retire early. He wanted no other ears when the moment came to begin his delicate exploration of Tsien's deepest feelings about the United States.

He bowed to the guard who gave him a careful visual check, and went up the covered walkway past the guest houses. It seemed he had run an endless maze of corridors when he finally emerged on the final courtyard that faced the main house. He could hear sounds of activity inside.

Tsien shook his hand tightly and Chang bowed to the older man. He was led, amid a flurry of questions and comments about his vacation and good works at the Canton conference, into the main living room where he was introduced to all the many members of the family and to three instructors from the university.

"How did you ever come to meet this strange man you've brought?" Tsien asked finally while he poured Chang a cup of *Kaoliang*.

Chang took several careful sips of the beverage before answering, weighing the proper inflections and the appropriate degree of casualness in his reply. "My bicycle broke a chain near his village, and when I went into the commune to find some tools, they offered a bowl of rice. I suppose they were impressed by my clothing. The head of the commune began chatting with me, quite freely. He talked about the *I Ching* and asked whether or not I believed in the fortunes the hexagrams told me. I told him no, that China had had enough of those who pretended to see into the future and that the *I Ching* was vulnerable to individual interpretation."

Tsien poured himself another drink and sat down, cross-legged. "Go on," he said.

Chang dropped some of the formality of his tone. "Then he told me of a young peasant who in his free hours would amuse the children of the farm by causing a needle, floating on the surface of a bowl of water, to spin violently, even when he was some distance away. I suspected a hidden lodestone or some other trick, but I asked to be allowed to meet him. An hour later he was brought to me, a filthy fellow, perhaps in his late thirties, named Shuang Daw-tse. He had brought his 'magic pin' with him and he asked for a bowl of water. He carefully floated the needle so that it was supported by surface tension. Then he asked me whether I was left or right handed. 'Right,' I said. Then he stared at the needle and it began to revolve to the right. For the rest of the afternoon I sat watching as the man stopped and started the needle, altering its velocity or direction at will."

"Fascinating." Tsien reached for a cigarette and placed it in a carved ivory holder. "This man, this Shuang, was he aware of the paranormality of his 'trick'?"

"No, I don't think he ever gave it much thought. But he apparently has a strong natural Psi Factor, so I brought him to you for testing. Perhaps he'd make a good student. At any rate you will be able to meet him tomorrow. Or tonight, if you wish."

"The morning will be soon enough. And the Canton meeting?"

Chang was grateful for the change of subject. They chatted about the general topics of the meeting with Chang holding back information about areas of mutual interest with, "I'll have to go into that later," hoping the withheld data would give him an excuse for an after-dinner stroll in the garden with Dr. Tsien.

To a Western eye, the main dining room was lavishly over-decorated. Everywhere were scrolls, paintings, and bronze figures. Dr. Tsien pointed to one painting, "Have you seen this one before? It's by Shoshi, called 'On the Way to the Fields.' I found it at the Albanian Arts Exhibition in Peking." They found their places amid a tasteful arrangement of Chinese court furniture of highly polished cherrywood. The table was decorated with fire-red flowers and was heavy with food arranged on a series of "lazy Susan" revolving trays which allowed guests their choice of a menu which must have run to more than a hundred separate dishes. *Kaoliang* flowed endlessly as they maneuvered their chopsticks and chatted quietly. Tsien's wife made a gracious hostess, and with each serving of a new delicacy, with each new beverage poured by the servants at a ritual signal, Chang felt himself caught up again in the venerable traditions of China. The graceful mannerisms, the exchange of flowery compliments, humbly expressing gratitude for the food and admiration for the host and hostess. Sadly, Chang found himself enjoying the evening.

Tsien was in good spirits and, as the evening wore on, Chang thought he detected a growing intoxication in his speech and his hearty laughter at the trivial jokes of his guests. And as the guests began to depart, relatives to their respective houses on the grounds, others to their guest cottages, each bowing humbly and thanking Tsien again for his munificent hospitality, Chang stood to one side and waited.

After the last guest had disappeared into the darkened courtyard, Chang and Tsien strolled alone through the formal garden. Each carried a cup of *Kaoliang*. Tsien held one arm behind him, walked with bowed head. At one point he paused to pick up a scrap of paper.

"I was immensely surprised to hear that you were cutting off your vacation to return to work," Tsien said pleasantly. "I know you were very tired after that last week of ours."

"The peasant Shuang Daw-tse might become one of our most promising students. I knew you would want to examine him as soon as possible."

"Ah, yes. Our work must proceed. And quickly, if we

are to be successful. You did well, Chang. I am proud of you. So is your country."

Chang sipped from his cup, letting the *Kaoliang* burn down to his stomach. How to get into it? How to bring the subject around to America? He decided to let himself appear a little drunk. Being careful to slur a word or two, he said finally, "Yes, our work is going well. How glad you must be that you returned to our land so many years ago."

"I no longer even think about my days in America. My treatment there was despicable. It is a great country, but it is in the hands of evil and decadent men."

"But haven't you ever wondered what your life might have been like if you had remained?"

"Oh, yes, sometimes, Chang. But you have no idea how difficult it would have been to convince the United States government to provide research funds for a project like ours. They expect results from science but they refuse to pay for the thought on which it must feed. They are so materialistic that I am told they now prefer color television to intelligent conversation. A typical American would far rather be given the wrong answer to a problem than to spend a few hours of thought arriving at the correct one. And he would far rather *watch* a professional sporting event than train himself to take part in one."

"But not all Americans are like that." Chang was treading near the edge. He hoped that his feigned drunkenness would excuse it.

"Oh, of course not. You yourself must have known many worthwhile individual Americans before your own defection, as did I. But surely every criminal must have many worthwhile brain cells, yet his behavior is dictated by an aberrent minority. So it is with nations."

The words struck a sudden echo in Chang's mind. A conversation with Moser about Bernadette's book, *A Nation's Brain.* Now Tsien made the thesis of a Bryn Mawr co-ed sound like the wisdom of Confucius. "Has K'ang Sheng uncovered any more information about that American plot he spoke of?"

"Nothing. Nothing at all. But we will hear of it when

his office has arrived at all the facts—and the proof. They'll get it, too. Did you know that K'ang Sheng is the highest-ranking intelligence chief in the entire world, that his department employs one man for every twenty-five hundred citizens? He'll uncover it. I, for one, believe it. The evil men of the world have grown fearful of China."

"Is that why you chose never to return to America?"

Tsien smiled and raised his cup in a toast. "Such questions, Chang. Perhaps you have had too much *Kaoliang*. To go back to America would be out of the question for me now. What could they offer me? Money? Hah!" He waved his free hand to indicate his expansive home. "I have here what few men—and no mere scientist—could hope to have in America. Freedom? I am as free as anyone here. I'm free to undertake my own research projects, free to spend as much money as I must on new programs and scientific endeavor. No, Chang, America holds nothing for me except hatred and violence."

Chang broke off his questioning. He had found no chink in Tsien's armor of dedication to China, no soft spot in his wall of hatred for America. If he could be made to return, persuasion would not be the force to do it.

"It's getting late, my friend," Tsien said as they had made a full round of the garden. "Let us retire, and tomorrow morning we will see about this unusual fellow you've discovered."

* * *

The dormitory and laboratory section of the main building of the University of Peking was V-shaped, with all scientific activity carried on in one leg and residence quarters for instructors and students maintained in the other. The top floor was for visitors. Tsien's office was at the point of the "V." Shuang Daw-tse was quartered down the long hallway, seven doors away.

Once escorted to his room, Shuang was left alone. A young private of the People's Liberation Army brought him food and tea, looked at him quizzically and left. Shuang tried to sleep but could only lie on his cot, staring at the ceiling. Agent Davis never left his mind. The resolute look in his eyes as he recognized the men he had been instructed to meet, the sudden action he had to take, even though he knew it could only end in his own death. Shuang wondered if the next hours would ask such a sacrifice of him. And whether he could answer with the same calm bravery.

So far everything had been easy. Almost too easy. Chang, of course, had made that possible. With his perfect cover, his high position, the *entry* would naturally have been easy. But how about the *escape?* Easy for Chang? Probably. In fact, Chang might not even need to escape. He was no paint and latex Chinese. He was real. Only an autopsy could detect the bones of Ben Garcia beneath the skin of Chang Kwok-wah. He had no recent espionage activity to be uncovered either. It had been years since he had even contacted the CIA, save for the one covert trip. As a matter of fact, he could simply turn Shuang Daw-tse over to the authorities and become a national hero—the mastermind of one of the wiliest kidnap plots in the history of espionage.

"Come on," Shuang said aloud, trying to push the thought from his mind. It was a monstrous idea. And yet in this crazy world it wasn't out of the question, either. The Chinese *did* want proof of the Talbot Agreement. Chang had said so himself. And who else could get it for them so quickly? "Here, gentlemen, is Captain James Moser, the man of whom I told you. He not only has been made a party to the Talbott Agreement but he was a long-time leader in their infamous 'Little Shanghai' project and is now deeply involved in their DEIMOS investigations." Ridiculous, he thought. There's no reason at all to question Chang's loyalty. Yet the doubt in his mind was reluctant to leave. How could he have walked past Davis that way without so much as a shrug of regret? Why did he arrange to see Tsien tonight alone? His mind whirled in disobedient conjecture. Then, suddenly—who else could have known that Bernadette was at Walker's Cay?

He jerked up in bed and started to rub his eyes, fighting back the hideous dream. Then he stopped himself as he sensed the delicate cosmetic fold of his eyelid. The inserts in his nose were beginning to hurt. And the plastic above his top molars chaffed at his gums and jaw. But nothing hurt as much as the worm of suspicion that bored into his mind.

Without knocking, Chang opened the door. Shuang dropped his head and closed his eyes to hide the thoughts behind them.

"He won't budge," Chang said as he walked over to the bed. "He's too old and tired, too set in his dedication to China and hatred of us."

Shuang spoke carefully. "Then it's tomorrow morning?"

Chang nodded. "I've already obtained two passes for a university car. I'm to stay at my own residence this evening. They'll serve you breakfast in your room at eight and at nine I'll come to bring you to Tsien's office. Let's hope there's no one else in there."

Shuang lay back.

"There's just one thing, just one thing," Chang said, rocking his head from side to side.

"What's that?"

"I don't want to kill him."

Shuang sat up slowly, almost visibly holding back his thoughts. Tsien *was* Chang's friend. It could mean only that. "There may be no choice, Chang."

"Still, I'd like to try to take him with us, not kill him."

"Get him out against his will?"

"Look," Chang said. "He's still a human being, an old man trapped by his technology and by a government that fawns over him."

"I don't like it." Shuang had fought back another reply —about Davis being a human being, too.

"You like the idea of killing him?" Chang looked coldly at Shuang.

Could we both be having doubts? Shuang thought. "What the hell's gotten into you, Chang? That's what this is all about—getting rid of Tsien! Hell no, I don't like the idea."

Chang slouched on the bed, put his head in his hands, rubbing his forehead and temples. "Sorry," he said. "I'm tired, I guess, and so are you. It's not good for friends to quarrel. Not at a time like this. Let's get some sleep. Tomorrow may be a very long day." He rose and turned back. "Or a very short one."

He left the room, closing the door softly behind him. Shuang's mouth was dry with doubt and anxiety. He got up and reached for a glass of water from the table, swirling it in his mouth before swallowing. Then he turned off the light. And, finally, his thoughts.

*　　*　　*

Sunlight streamed through the open window. Shuang ate slowly. A bowl of rice, some fresh figs, and tea. It was almost an hour before he was to see Tsien. He had plenty of time. And it was time he would use to find a way out of a trap, if it was a trap. As he finished eating and as he sat later, silently staring at his chopsticks, he knew what he must do. At the slightest hint of any change in procedure, if Chang made the slightest misstep, or even if there were someone else in the office, he would kill Tsien himself if it took his last breath of life. And it would.

There was a tap on the door at a punctual five minutes before nine, and Chang entered, mumbling an apology for his behavior the night before. Together, they walked down the hall and entered Dr. Tsien's office. It was paneled in rich, rubbed oak with a thick green carpet that stretched from wall to wall and it commanded an impressive view of the city through a single wide window. Tsien's taste for beauty was reflected throughout in handsome wall tapestries and magnificent artifacts from an older, freer, and more creative China. Through a door, Shuang could see a corner of Tsien's laboratory, bulging with electronic instruments.

Chang introduced Shuang to Tsien immediately. The older man smiled benevolently at the peasant and closed the door to his office. He sat down behind the desk, picked up a silver letter opener and gestured toward Shuang. "We can talk here in complete privacy. Please sit down," he said. "First, let me ask you if you would mind subjecting yourself to some tests."

Shuang looked up, mute. Now, he thought. Right off. Don't waste time with pleasantries. He looked at Chang and felt that he was thinking the same thing. He felt a sudden panic in his chest and abdomen. His tongue felt thick in his mouth. He fought it free, sweat growing ominously on his forehead and chest. Jim Moser stared at Tsien and said, "I think Chang Kwok-wah has something to tell you." He spoke in English.

Tsien was stunned. He glared at the peasant in disbelief, letting the silver letter opener fall from his stiffened fingers. "You speak English?"

Silence. Moser turned his head toward Chang, but kept the letter opener within his peripheral vision. He watched as Chang rose slowly. "Dr. Tsien, he speaks English because he is an American."

"What is this?" Tsien's voice faltered as he half rose from his chair. "I don't believe—"

"It's true, Dr. Tsien." Chang took a defiant step toward him. "Now, if you will sit down I shall tell you a story. I think you will find it easier if you are seated."

The older man sat again, glancing between the two Oriental faces. He looked at the telephone on his desk but, at the same moment, Chang casually slid it out of his reach. Then he sat on the edge of the desk and Moser stepped over next to him.

"Dr. Tsien, I am here to implore you to return to the United States."

"You are American? *You*, Chang?"

"Both of us are, and we are here with the strongest suggestion that you return with us."

Tsien was still in something very close to the medical definition of shock, clammy sweat bathing his paled face. He stared incredulously at Chang. "You've been an agent all along. For all those years we worked together." He glanced at Moser. "Who are you? You're not Chinese."

"No, I'm not, Dr. Tsien, nor is Chang actually," Moser said, "but this is not the place to go into it. You *must* return with us."

With that, Tsien began to tremble. The old man was frightened and Chang felt sorry for him. He wished that Moser hadn't been so abrupt, so cold.

"That's impossible! You'll never get out of China."

Moser answered with measured words. "That doesn't matter, Doctor. We are here to get *you* out."

There was only a moment's pause. "Or to see you killed."

Tsien shook his head, still unbelieving. "I cannot go. I will not go. You men are both mad. You'll never get out of here!" He lunged forward and reached across the desk for the telephone. Moser chopped fiercely at his wrist. Tsien fell back, wincing in pain. "Pigs!" he shouted. "Sons of capitalist swine! China will annihilate you—and your Russian brothers. You ask me to return to *your* country, to that kennel where I was treated worse than a Chinese dog? To the country that whipped me like a beggar after I had given them everything, helped them win their capitalist war?"

Tsien's knee had edged open the top drawer of the desk. In the next instant he had reached in for an automatic pistol. Moser leaped, chopping savagely at his arm. Tsien cursed and fumbled to get a grip on the weapon. Moser got his arm, vaulting the desk and twisting the arm behind his back, raising his knee sharply upward. Tsien cursed again, tried to twist free. Then Moser wrenched Tsien's neck into the crook of his right arm. The gun clattered free on the desk top. Chang picked it up and dropped it into his pocket. Then it happened. Tsien stiffened with a surge of iron strength, almost breaking Moser's hold. Then he went limp. As Moser relaxed his right arm, Tsien slid slowly to the carpeted floor.

Chang was beside him immediately, loosening his collar, feeling his chest. Moser took Tsien's wrist and felt for a pulse. Chang put his ear to his chest. There was no breathing. No pulse. "He's dead," Moser whispered. "I didn't hold him that tightly. His heart?"

"Probably," Chang said softly. "My God."

Moser put his hand on the old man's forehead, felt again for a sign of life. Chang was picking up the papers that had fallen to the rug. He pointed to the laboratory door. "Let's take him in there."

At that moment the office door swung open and a university guard stepped into the room, his eyes opening wide with shock. He saw Moser kneeling over Tsien and reached for the rifle on his shoulder. Chang leveled the automatic at him.

"Lower the rifle," Moser snapped in Mandarin. "Make one sound and you're dead."

He stepped up and took the rifle from the guard and closed the door quietly. He shoved the guard toward the center of the room with the barrel of the rifle. "Don't shoot him," Chang said in English. "You'll have every student in the place down on us."

"Turn around," Moser ordered, prodding the soldier again. When he did, Moser swung the rifle butt up with a grunt, hitting the side of his head hard. The soldier crumpled.

"Get him, Chang."

Moser immediately began dragging Tsien's lifeless body toward the laboratory. Inside, he stuffed him into a closet. Chang was struggling with the unconscious guard. "He'll be out for quite a while," Moser said. He went to a table and picked up a lamp. With the cord, he bound the guard's arms tightly behind his back. Chang found a roll of electrical tape in the lab and secured his feet. Moser took the rag from his pocket, stuffed it into the guard's mouth and then taped it shut.

"Can we lock that door from the inside as we leave?" he asked Chang.

Chang checked the lock. Yes, they could. They checked the room once again. It would pass a casual inspection. "Okay," Moser said finally, "let's go."

They locked the door and left the room. Down the hall two students were chatting by a water fountain. On the second floor they passed an instructor. Chang greeted him in passing.

Outside, they walked down the university stairs and toward the guardhouse. Two cars were parked nearby.

Chang signaled Moser into one of them and went over to present his passes and the order for the later model car.

The guard looked over the papers and picked up the telephone. "Dr. Tsien won't be in his office, if that's who you're calling," Chang said evenly. "He's probably on his way to the main laboratory now."

The guard didn't acknowledge Chang's comment and dialed the phone. He listened for several rings. No one answered. Chang let his irritation show, slamming his open palm against the window ledge. "Come on," he barked. "I don't have the time for your silly protocol!"

The sound of authority flustered the guard. He looked at Chang, fumbled with the passes, and finally handed him the keys to the 1962 Vauxhall.

Chang got in and started the engine. He turned the wheel slowly and guided the compact car carefully out the gate. Then he turned left and headed for the road to Tientsin. Once out of the city, the road turned to little more than a rutted path, a single dirt-surfaced lane of muddy chuckholes meandering around rice fields and communal farms. They passed village after nameless village, each filled to the choking point with hundreds of hungry, nameless peasants.

"I give them no more than two hours to discover him," Chang said. "Somebody is sure to be phoning him and eventually they'll go look."

"Then let's step on it," Moser said. "Tientsin's about a four-hour drive, isn't it?"

"Probably more on this road," Chang said as they bounced along, the Vauxhall's engine whining in complaint at the ruts and potholes. "And they're going to be looking for this car as well as for us." Moser looked at the automatic Chang had given him. It was an old Mauser 7.65. He slipped the clip back, pulled back the receiver. The chamber was empty but the clip held nine shells. Dr. Tsien was a foolish genius, he thought. He never could have cocked the gun in time to hurt anyone. Then he checked the safety action and clicked the receiver shut, a round in the chamber.

More than three hours later and some ten miles west of

Tientsin, the car was still shuddering and pitching at full speed. The road was a little better, parallel to a long straight irrigation ditch. It was drier country now without marshes. Then, as it topped a low rise a few hundred yards ahead, they saw a truck approaching. It was a military patrol. "This is it," Moser said.

"Let's hope not," Chang said as the truck stopped ahead of them, blocking the road. "But maybe this is our chance to switch."

They came to a slow stop a hundred feet from the truck. Moser watched as three men got out of the dun-colored wagon. Each carried a rifle but left them slung on their shoulders. "They haven't heard yet," he said.

"Get out," Chang said, "and act friendly. Don't let them see the gun until they're close." Moser opened the door and Shuang Daw-tse, the cowering peasant, took a few steps forward. Chang got out the other side and they both stood in front of the Vauxhall, waiting for the guards.

The leader yelled at them in Mandarin, "Let me see your papers."

Chang began fumbling in his *Jem-ming* as the guards drew closer. "Why are you stopping us?" Chang asked in a sharp tone. "We are on official business." The guard mumbled something about routine. "I am Chang Kwok-wah from the university," Chang continued, waving his papers.

As the lead guard reached out to take the papers, Chang brought his fist up quickly and caught him on the jaw. At the same moment, two shots rang from Moser's gun and Chang saw another guard drop, still reaching for the strap of his rifle. His man had staggered back and now Chang was on him, kicking him in the groin. He looked up. The third guard had been well in the rear. Now he was running toward Chang, bayoneted rifle forward. Another shot sang from the opposite side of the car. The guard stiffened, head back, with his rifle pointing crazily to one side. But he kept on running, finally flopping prone almost at Chang's feet. Chang grabbed the loose rifle and plunged the bayonet through his back, withdrew it and then slashed its point into the belly of the first guard. He shrieked once and then the road was quiet.

Moser ran over to him. "Let's get their pants and jackets off before they get bloody," he said. "Maybe they won't be looking for a couple of AWOL soldiers."

"Good," Chang answered. "But they're going to be looking for everything and everybody before too long." They pulled the thick military jackets and pants over their own clothes. Then they stuffed the bodies into the rear seat of the Vauxhall and Moser started it, slammed it into low gear and guided it into the canal. It sank with a hiss of steam, completely hidden just below the surface of the brown water.

Moser jumped up into the driver's side of the truck. Chang was wearing the jacket of the ranking man so he would not be the driver. He jockeyed the clumsy vehicle around on the narrow road, and they wove again down the road to Tientsin. Chang was fiddling with the collar of the dingy jacket. It was too small for him. Moser kept his eyes trained on the road ahead, watching for the checkpoint to the city.

Chang went through the glove compartment and checked behind the seat for anything of use. He took a flashlight from a clip below the dash, tested it and stuck it in his pocket. There were several tags, the vehicle registration, a military instruction manual but no maps.

Then Moser spotted the checkpoint ahead, a red-and-white striped railroad crossing bar blocking the road. Beside it a small stucco guardhouse stood blandly in the sun, and he could see the edges of two trucks parked behind it. Moser shifted down and approached slowly. He hung his elbow out the window so that they could see his uniform, maybe wave them through.

Instead a guard ran out of the stucco house. He turned back toward the parked trucks and waved his arm. Seconds later, men began running up behind him, rifles ready. "More of them," Moser said. "I'm going through."

Twenty feet from the gate Moser jammed the truck into low gear and stomped down on the accelerator. The truck lurched forward with a whine, splintering the thin, candy-striped railing and sending the soldiers diving for cover. But they were up and firing as Moser speed-shifted to second and picked up speed down the better road past the guard shack.

Moser swerved the clumsy truck from side to side, trying to present as hard a target as possible. A bullet cracked into the rearview mirror, shattering the glass and another ricocheted off the side of the cab, clipping off the side mirror. Then the front window was hit, splintering into a spidery network. Moser shifted into high. He turned to Chang. "Keep your head—" His words choked as Chang turned toward him, eyes wide, as a sudden red splash washed across his cheek. His expression froze, his flesh torn away and thrown against the dashboard. He dropped forward. What was left of his head flopped on his knee, the white bone showing where his jaw had been. One arm dropped down and swung lifelessly, dangling like a broken wire. Moser couldn't call out. Suddenly he was sick, a vomit of half-digested rice regurgitating into his mouth. He swallowed. He heard a thumping against the firewall and looked over. It was Chang's leg, jerking against it in violent electric spasms.

He sped on.

*   *   *

Tientsin had changed little since pre-Communist days. Except for militia troops, the Red Guard, and the new nihilism that clouded the eyes of the people, it was the Tientsin of old, retaining the international flavor from the days when it was the center for trade delegations from many nations. Moser thought it looked like pictures of Shanghai. Despite the throngs of hopeless people, despite the stinking slums and filthy side-streets, he could feel the livelier air of worldliness around him, the amorphous atmosphere that seems to link the coastal cities of every nation.

Moser left the bicycle he had stolen in an alley and walked along the dirty streets toward the downtown sector. He had ditched the truck and uniform as soon as he reached the outskirts and was now a peasant again, walking hunched and faceless through the crowds.

Alone. Without Chang's wisdom and friendship to warm and comfort him. Chang. His friend, whom he had accused in his mind of evil and disloyalty, his friend who lay crumpled on the seat of a rusted army truck, dead. A canal ditch his burial site, a hulk of ancient sheet metal his casket, a single peasant to mourn for him.

Moser's shuffling gait was even slower now. The momentum of his flight to freedom was lost, almost within sight of his goal. He thought of how Chang must have felt in Macao—almost free but somehow loathe to take the last, desperate step. He fought back at his despair, trying to think of nothing but the rendezvous with the "Westridge."

But Davis was gone, and there was no boat. Chang was gone, and there was no one to guide him to the harbor. He had no compass—it was missing from Chang's pockets, probably lost during the struggle by the canal. Only a battered flashlight. He looked at the hazy afternoon sky and hoped that the night would be clear. He was going to need the stars.

Moser trudged on, a growing hunger stabbing at him. But he was afraid to ask for food. His dialect would surely mark him as a stranger. True, scholars classified the speech of Tientsin as Mandarin, but how different it would sound compared to the haughty accents of Peking. The local speech, spiced by generations of sailors from up and down the coast, was flecked with intonations of *Wu, Hakka,* and even far-off Cantonese. But he knew he would eventually have to speak to someone. He rehearsed phrases, half-aloud, trying to give them a feeble sound that might cover up his faulty accent.

Then he wondered about his makeup, his hair. Were his brown roots showing yet? Rub on a little carbon paper, the doctor said. Would the good doctor kindly tell him where to find a sheet of carbon paper on the squalid streets of Tientsin? He brushed his fingers nervously across his face. At least he couldn't feel a beard yet.

He kept walking, the sun to his back, until he had

passed through the heart of the city. Now the crowds of faceless poor were beginning to thin out, and with them Moser's protection. Right now, he thought, I'd be better off inside. The militia, the Red Guard, everyone must be searching for him by now. Perhaps the soldier in Tsien's office had a photographic memory and was able to describe him perfectly. Every glance from a passerby, every casual look from a stranger, made him shudder now. Get indoors, Moser. Can't let your mind start playing tricks.

There was a rank bar straight ahead. Moser thought he could smell it before he reached the doorway. He slouched inside, blinked his eyes against the dimness, groped his way to a filthy corner table. He looked up toward the bar. Three whores were fussing over a drunken man, professionally exploring his crotch, trying to excite him. But the hulk only sat in a stupor. Tiring of the game, one of the trio looked around the room, her gaze stopping at his table. He looked away. Around the foul, dim room a dozen patrons were scattered, eating from greasy bowls. He smelled rice. It tantalized him.

The disheveled waiter scuffed over to his table and asked what he wanted, eyeing him suspiciously. Moser hesitated, looking, if anything, more suspicious, more conspicuously self-conscious. "Rice," he said at last, trying in a single word to mimic the man's dialect. He dropped his glance to the table top. A bug crawled across it.

Time. What time was it? He looked up at the bar. An old clock on a high shelf read four-thirty. Five and a half hours to go. He had to get a boat soon, had to get to the wharves and steal one and then, somehow, find the elusive Point Sierra.

But, God, he didn't even know how to get to the port settlement. He didn't know the channel or the tides and currents of the marsh-ringed harbor. Yet he had to calculate time and distance accurately, allowing for currents and drift. For the first time in years he tried to recall his earliest training in the days before the Navy had made him a classroom captain.

The waiter brought him rice and tea in chipped and stained bowls. He sucked down the rice eagerly, paying for it with coupons he had taken from Chang's *Jem-ming*. Then he sipped at the tea and tried to relax. He must appear calm, natural, not too humble nor too brash—the unnoticed, invisible man. He watched the whores again, still unsuccessfully pawing the drunk. One looked straight at him and smiled. She couldn't have been more than sixteen, Moser thought. She turned on the stool and spread her hands along the inside of her thighs and moved her tongue between her half-closed lips. He sipped his tea and returned her gaze, almost accidentally. In a moment she was sliding in beside him, resting her hand on his leg. "You come upstairs with me, my handsome friend, and we will have a nice time."

Moser shook his head. "I have no money." He smiled weakly.

"Only ten *yuan*," she cajoled, pressing her hand up his leg.

"That is very reasonable, but I have just arrived in the city and truly have no money," he said. "I am to work soon in a textile mill."

"Am I not pretty?"

"Of a beauty such as I am not used to," he said. Then he thought of the wharves. "I have relatives who live by the sea," he went on. "I could get money from them. Can you tell me how to get there?"

She obliged, greedily, and he promised to return later. As he left the bar the sun was sinking behind the hills.

Mingling with the crowds in the narrow streets, he wound his way out of the slum and into a smoky industrial area. Streams of yellow smoke curled into the twilight sky and he could smell sulphur burning. Now and then a truckload of Red Guards would rumble through the streets but no one looked at the anonymous peasant. He was only one man in what seemed to Moser like the entire population of China, converging on this one city. People were everywhere, still working at a hundred slow, manual tasks. Children darted from every doorway, even at this hour, and the old and sick slouched against every wall or simply lay unnoticed in the streets. A group of young teenagers passed, strutting proudly as they sang Mao songs and waved banners.

Moser walked faster under the protection of the darkening sky. The asphalt, still blistering from the heat of the day, radiated an oppressive warmth with every step.

At the end of an hour he was walking along a canal that was to lead him to the port settlement of Tangku. On one side the marshes stretched far away, cross-hatched with canals. Working by torchlight, a gang of laborers was digging a drainage ditch to reclaim more land, aiding the government in its quest for more trade with Britain and Canada. Moser guessed at the time and hurried on.

The wharf in Tangku was a sea of junks, sampans, and flimsy boats of no discernible type. In a shop window along the wharf he saw a clock, dimly lit by a small lamp. It was eight-thirty. He had about half an hour to find a boat.

His legs were damp and cramped from walking and he struggled down the wooden steps toward the quay. At the bottom, a sharp click stopped him abruptly. A beam of light hit him squarely in the face. His hands went up to his eyes, involuntarily, and he heard a raspy voice shout at him. The light moved down and he saw two guards with rifles silhouetted against the dimming sky. One of them held a large club, high and ready for work. The other demanded his papers. Moser noticed no one else around. The shore seemed deserted.

As the guards approached, he kept his arms innocently at his sides. The guard on the left took a step forward and Moser suddenly brought his stiffened right palm upward, jabbing the fingers under the man's rib cage. He grunted and staggered backward, choking for breath. The other guard, club still raised, lunged forward, slashing at him with the heavy cudgel. Moser felt it graze his cheek and shoulder as he twisted out of the way. The blow jarred his teeth. He tasted blood. But now his body was performing almost without his conscious mind, going through the judo exercises he had practiced so long ago. It was as if he had been put under the command of a for-

gotten corner of his brain that was now sending light-
ning-fast orders to every muscle.

The club's momentum had brought the guard down to
a stooping position as he missed his target, and now the
target's knee smashed upward into his face. Then he
jerked up, holding his crushed nose, trying desperately to
see. But, like a matador going in over the horns, Moser
jabbed two fingers into the spongy eyes. The man
screamed and dropped to his knees. Then Moser's right
foot caught his head, bashing it silent against the concrete
abutment. Now the other guard was on his back, his arm
tightening around Moser's neck. Then an elbow shot
backward, quickly, into the man's stomach and, as the
death-grip loosened, Moser whirled and brought his knee
into the man's groin. He sucked in air with a gurgling sound
and fell voiceless to the ground.

Moser picked up the club and brought it down on the
man's head and, leaving both men limp, jumped down to
the end of the quay. He waited a moment, still trembling
uncontrollably from the exertion. Had anyone heard?
Was anyone coming? But there was only silence. If anyone had noticed the shrieks of pain, they had noticed too
that the pain was not their own, and had gone about their
business or their sleep with the timeless impassivity of the
Oriental.

In front of Moser, a string of colored lights marked the
location of the tethered sampans. Beyond, a distorted
orange crescent was climbing out of the coastal waters,
trying to make a moon. Moser walked along a sloshing,
lurching gangway, cutting his fingers as he steadied himself on a sharp supporting wire. Somewhere in the night
he heard a boat whistle. On one of the junks, a baby was
crying.

He walked quietly along the tilting boards, looking for a
quiet junk, an empty sampan. But there seemed to be
lights in all of them, flickering in a quiet vigil through the
lonely China night. He couldn't risk disturbing a family,
face the squawking and screaming of the women. But he
had to have a boat.

Then, near the end of the long quay, he saw a smaller

craft, barely more than a canvas-covered whale-boat, swaying and bobbing in the waves. He stepped toward it carefully. No lights.

Moser grabbed the craft's gunwale and pulled it gently to him. He craned his neck inside. Darkness. Then, reaching in under the protection of the canvas, he flicked on the flashlight, holding the automatic ready in the other hand. There was a form on a plank cot. It stirred.

He was aboard with a lightfooted vault. *"Hung-hao!"* he whispered urgently. "Be quiet!"

The man raised his head and looked at him with unexpected calm. "Who are you?" the man said evenly. "What do you want?"

"I need your help," Moser said, desperately. "You must take me out into the bay."

The man blinked in the flashlight glare and shook his head slowly. "That I may not do," he said. "Please leave my boat and go away."

Moser let the outline of the automatic fall within the circle of light. "Take me out," he hissed.

The man looked at the gun. "Where did you get that? If they find it they will kill you!"

"Never mind," Moser said, staring at a face that might have been no more than fifty or fifty-five years old, but it bore a resolute wisdom gained from years of living in the stress and slavery of modern China. "Let's get going," he commanded.

The man pointed at the gun and smiled. "Put your gun away, young man. I'm much too old and tired to be afraid of it. But why do you want to go out on the sea at night?"

"I'll tell you later," Moser urged. "Now hurry!" The man moved up to start his small, asthmatic motor and then sat down at the tiller as Moser cast off. They moved slowly out into the bay.

The man looked at Moser as he took a seat a few feet away from his. "You have not told me why it is you escape. So I will tell you. You escape air that does not refresh your lungs. You escape a land that works but does not create. You escape a fear so constant that you are driven to fearless, foolish acts in running from it. But how can you succeed?"

Moser listened as the man talked, glancing skyward and shoreward, trying to fix his position with the lights of Tangku, the dark headlands to the south, and the flickering north light of Polaris, the tail of Ursa Minor. He motioned him to bear to starboard.

"It may be foolish, good man, but I must succeed," Moser said, trying to mimic his speech, not to deceive the man but to make himself understood.

"I wish I had your youth," the man said, bowing his head.

Moser studied him. A fisherman, surely. But his wife and family? Dead, perhaps? Or taken by the soldiers to further the cause of the Great Proletarian Cultural Revolution. And the man? Still young by Western standards, he was cast aside. Yet he stays alive, stays sane, even stays hopeful, Moser thought, despite a stranger who prods him from his sleep at gunpoint.

"What place do you seek?" the man said suddenly. Moser explained the triangulation by which he hoped to find Point Sierra and they stared skyward together. Then the man looked down. "A little more this way," he said. Then, without a signal from Moser, he cut the engine. "We are here," he announced. "And what place is this?"

Moser looked around, checking their position. They were as close to Point Sierra as his memory of the charts could bring them, maybe closer, because the man had brought a deeper knowledge of the stars to bear on their problems of navigation. "You're not afraid of me at all, are you?" Moser asked gently.

"No, I do not fear you," the man said. "Life here is fearful enough. They have taken from me everything that can be taken. I can only receive. Death would be a gift. But you cannot understand that, can you?"

"Yes, I can," Moser said. He looked around impatiently. They had been drifting a long time.

"It is very difficult to understand, I think," the man said, "for one who is not Chinese."

Moser turned. "What?"

"I know," the man said. "In my life I have heard many voices." Moser only stared, trying to think of a way to answer.

Then he heard it. A hundred yards away, no more, the sound of gurgling water, a quick stirring of the surface, and the smooth black hull rising in a moon-splashed foam. The "Westridge."

Moser's chest hammered with excitement. He was going to make it. For the first time since he hit the beach at Tsingtao, he thought of Washington. The President. Bernadette.

The submarine leveled itself in the water. In seconds a dull light glowed from the conning tower. "Head for that light," he said to the man.

"What is it?"

"A submarine from America," Moser said intensely. "I am an American. That is why I had to force you to take me here." He felt in his pocket for the revolver, Dr. Tsien's revolver. He lifted it out by the muzzle and tossed in into the sea. Then he brought out the flashlight he had taken from the body of Chang Kwok-wah. Moser blinked the beam toward the submarine.

In moments they were alongside the "Westridge" and Hodges was climbing out on the deck. Someone tossed them a manrope.

"Come on," Hodges yelled down. "Let's get the hell out of here."

Suddenly the man in the boat grabbed Moser. "Take me with you," he said. "Please take me to America."

Moser turned, flashlight still burning in his hand. The light hit the old man's face, weatherbeaten from the sea and from life. It was wet with tears. "Please," he said again, almost inaudibly.

Moser turned toward the sub. "Take this man up first."

Hodges called down, "Where's Chang?"

"Dead. Take this man aboard."

"You know I can't do that," Hodges snapped.

"Hodges," he yelled, "take him up!"

"Who is he, Moser? I can't take an unauthorized person aboard!"

"God damn it, Hodges, take him aboard!"

Hodges finally waved to the crewmen and they hustled the man aboard the "Westridge." Moser climbed up swiftly behind them and stood next to Hodges.

"Listen," Hodges said, "what are you trying to do?"

"He saved my life," Moser said with finality and then turned abruptly away as he watched the men help the Chinese down the hatch.

"We can't take refugees back with us," Hodges said.

Moser stared at him, a hard, unrelenting stare that was clearly legible even in the hazy moonlight. He turned to look out over the cold black water to the Chinese mainland beyond. "Why not?" he asked in a murmur, still staring out. "We left one of ours with them, didn't we?"

He turned again and went below, Hodges behind him. A crewman spun a handle, someone barked an order, and the "Westridge" slid silently into the black, protecting sea.

Inside the sub, he remembered Ben Garcia. Moser was out of China now, and he could weep.

Other award books you'll enjoy . . .

THE JOHNNY FEDORA ESPIONAGE SERIES

JOHNNY GOES WEST . . on a mission that begins in a dingy London hovel and ends in screaming terror in the jungles of Venezuela. A324—60¢

FERAMONTOV . . brings Johnny closer to the most ingenious triple cross a cruel beauty could desire.

A322—75¢

TIMELOCK . . holds Johnny in a leaden vise—trapped by a Spanish torturer and by his own amnesia! A343—75¢

MOUNTAINHEAD . . in the Himalayas—where Johnny must find the answers behind a mysterious plane crash and its scheming survivors. A373—60¢

TRIESTE . . hides a diabolical Communist plot, which Johnny must uncover in a deadly race against time.

A394—60¢

HIGH REQUIEM . . sounds for Johnny when he goes to a super-secret base in the African desert where a saboteur is loose and the ultimate destructive weapon is at stake. A408—60¢

DEAD MEN ALIVE . . takes Johnny to darkest Africa to find a man where no one has survived before and five men and a fiery blonde come along to turn the mission into a bloody nightmare. A447—60¢

THE GENTLEMEN AT LARGE

A bizarre trap is sprung when the British Government assigns *The Gentlemen* to smash a ruthless spy ring.

A332—60¢

THE GENTLEMEN REFORM

Operation Jailbreak was *The Gentlemen's* most dangerous mission—no man had ever escaped from the maximum security prison and lived to brag about it!

A331—60¢

Two Exciting Novels by John Boland!

TIGER SQUADRON
Ira Jones
The brave men who hurled back Goering's Luftwaffe to bring England to shining victory.
A210—75¢

THE RIVER WAR
Winston S. Churchill
The exact military details of the reconquest of the Egyptian Sudan.
A123—75¢

HUNZA HEALTH SECRETS
Renee Taylor
The secrets of lasting youth discovered in an amazing land where 100-year-old women and men live in vigorous physical and mental health.
A360—60¢

ISOMETRICS
Henry Wittenberg
The amazing new system of no-motion exercises for figure control.
A365—75¢

YOGA MADE EASY
Desmond Dunne
Take years off your face and figure; banish pain, anxiety and frustration—the ancient art of Yoga adapted for use by modern busy Americans.
A196—75¢